Praise for Natasha Moore's
The Passion-Minded Professor

"The Passion-Minded Professor is a wonderful love story that will draw you in right from the first page. Roxy and Daniel's chemistry (no pun intended) is so believable, you think you know these people in real life. I felt I was a part of the story all the way through it. I truly enjoyed The Passion-Minded Professor and I am Joyfully Recommending it."

~ *Vivian, Joyfully Reviewed*

Look for these titles by

Natasha Moore

Now Available:

The Ride of Her Life

The Passion-Minded Professor

Natasha Moore

A Samhain Publishing, Ltd. publication.

Samhain Publishing, Ltd.
577 Mulberry Street, Suite 1520
Macon, GA 31201
www.samhainpublishing.com

The Passion-Minded Professor

Print ISBN: 978-1-60504-177-3
Digital ISBN: 978-1-60504-181-0

Editing by Laurie Rauch
Cover by Angela Waters

First Samhain Publishing, Ltd. electronic publication: June 2008
First Samhain Publishing, Ltd. print publication: April 2009

Dedication

To Rhonda, Bren and Chell—thanks for everything.

To my editor, Laurie Rauch, for always helping me make my stories the best they can be.

Chapter One

Dangerous curves ahead.

What an odd thought to pop into his head. Uncharacteristic thoughts had to be recorded immediately. Dr. Daniel Jennings knew he should turn away from the image of a long-dead sex symbol standing in the doorway to his chem lab and make a note of his observations before he forgot them. His notebook was only two feet from him, but he found it impossible to look away.

Instead, he stood and stared at a clone of Marilyn Monroe, wondering what she was doing here in the college town of Cowden, New York. Unlike so many of the skinny students running around the Cowden State University campus, she had a woman's body beneath her bright red sweater and faded blue jeans. A body a man could sink into. Breasts a man could grab onto. Hips he could grind against and not worry about breaking.

What was he thinking?

"Is Gina here?" She didn't sound like Marilyn Monroe. Her voice was clear and bright, and not the least bit breathy. The wavy hair that fell to her shoulders was blonde, but it was a soft honey blonde, not a brassy platinum. Her mouth was wide, her lips red and shiny. Daniel swallowed as he stared at her mouth.

"Hello? Earth to Professor? Is Gina here?"

She was talking to him but her words seemed to echo in his head. He didn't even know what she said. He finally snapped out of whatever stupor he'd been in and drove his fingers through hair that needed to be cut weeks ago. What had just happened?

It must have been the potion.

The possibility that his formula was all he hoped it would be made his heart race. He'd never had such a strong, erotic reaction to a woman before. He'd never been rendered speechless by blonde hair, red lips, and luscious curves.

It had to be the potion.

"I have to write this down." Finally, he dragged his gaze away from the distracting young woman and strode to the notebook on his desk. "I have to record my reactions." And change all his plans for the experiment.

"Dr. Jennings?"

He glanced over his shoulder. She'd stepped into the lab. He pushed the papers around, frantically trying to locate his pencil. "You've ruined everything," he grumbled. He finally discovered the pencil beneath the test papers he should have been grading. He started scribbling in his notebook, using shorthand only he could understand. "This was supposed to be a controlled experiment."

"I'm sorry," she sighed dramatically, "if you didn't want anyone to walk in, you should have closed your door." She inched closer to his desk. "Closed the door and locked it."

He could smell her now, some kind of exotic scent he couldn't name. Was it a fragrance she sprayed on, or was that her own unique scent? He kept scribbling. He didn't need to know. He shouldn't even be wondering about it.

"What did I ruin?" she asked, peeking over his shoulder.

He glanced up at her. Big mistake. His face met her generous cleavage. He started to sweat and his cock twitched before he could look away from the curves of pale flesh.

He shifted in his seat to relieve the pressure. "Never mind. Just go away." He crossed out the references to her breasts. They wouldn't be necessary for the study. The trouble was, he couldn't think about anything but her breasts at the moment.

"I'm looking for Gina Manetti," she said. Her musical voice wrapped around his brain and squeezed out all coherent thought. She spoke slowly, as if she thought he was an imbecile or something. "Gina Manetti? She is your lab assistant, isn't she?"

Maybe he put too much on. He'd slapped the potion on like aftershave. Damn, he was close to sensory overload. After he made a note to lower the dose next time, he threw down the pencil in frustration.

Stupid. How could he be so stupid? He hadn't even measured how much he used tonight. A first-year student could have done a better job. It was just that when Gina asked if she could leave early, he decided to take advantage of the time alone and try it out.

That was no excuse. He knew how to run a proper experiment. He taught the technique, for heaven's sake. The problem was he hadn't been planning to test it in this way tonight. He'd simply wanted to make sure the liquid itself didn't cause any reaction to the skin. Make note of any initial reactions he had to the elixir itself. He hadn't planned on being in contact with any women tonight after Gina left.

Oh, Gina. Right. He studied the woman standing beside him now. She wasn't as young as he first thought. A grad student maybe, like Gina. Her face really wasn't at all like Marilyn Monroe's. Actually, she was much more attractive than the movie star ever was.

It must have been the hourglass figure that put the outrageous thoughts about sex symbols into his head. The figure he could vividly picture naked and sprawled upon his bed. Or on her knees in front of him, her slick mouth—

Daniel jumped out of his chair, as if that would stop the erotic images bombarding his brain. “I’m afraid you’ll have to go now.”

She hopped back, out of his way. “I said I was sorry. I just need to see Gina. She’s supposed to be here. Where is she?”

What happened to Gina? Oh, right. “She left half an hour ago.”

“Shit. She was going to give me a ride home.”

“I had the impression she had a hot date.”

She sighed. Daniel could see her mind working, the expression on her face changing from amusement to annoyance to acceptance. “Oh, well. It’s a nice evening for a walk. Thanks, Doc.”

Daniel glanced out the window. The autumn sky was dark and it wasn’t even six o’clock yet. “You can’t walk alone after dark.”

She rolled her eyes as if she was used to living dangerously. “Don’t worry about me, Professor. It’s not that far.”

“I’ll give you a ride. I was planning to leave soon anyway.”

Where did that come from? He had hours of work left. He never went home until it was time to fall into bed, where he’d collapse into exhausted sleep, and start all over again in the morning.

“No, that’s okay. You were in the middle of an experiment. One I apparently screwed up for you. You’ll probably have to start all over again.”

"No. I'm sorry. I shouldn't have blamed you for that. It was only preliminary testing. No harm done."

She put her hands on her hips and frowned. "How do I know I wouldn't be in more trouble getting into a car with you than walking across campus in the dark?"

He swore he could feel her gaze run along his skin as she looked him up and down. Daniel knew what she saw. The rumpled lab coat, the shaggy hair. Wire-rimmed glasses on a plain face. Certainly nothing to compare with the colorful woman who stood before him.

"I can assure you that I am perfectly harmless."

"Yeah, well, I don't know that I'd take your word for it," she told him, crossing her arms under her breasts. He *had* to stop thinking about her breasts. "But Gina speaks very highly of you. She thinks you're the smartest and nicest guy she's ever met."

A warm rush of surprise spread through him. "Gina said that?"

"Yeah. She also thinks you work too hard and are hiding away from the world up here in your lab."

"I take back all the nice things I've said about her," he grumbled.

"Hey, I'm her roommate. Who else is she going to tell these things to?"

"Gina's roommate?" Daniel struggled to place a name to the friend she'd mentioned to him occasionally. "Then you must be…?"

"Roxy Morgan." She held out her hand. "Nice to meet you, Dr. Jennings."

Her hand was warm, her handshake strong. Shivers of something he couldn't even describe shot through his body at her touch. He hadn't thought about what effect the potion might have on touch. He'd only thought about attraction. Sexual interest. But certainly touch was a part of that, wasn't it? He hadn't considered that before.

He rushed back to his notebook to add this new revelation to the study he was making on the attraction elixir he had developed.

What his big-mouthed lab assistant called a love potion.

Roxy watched Dr. Jennings scribble more words in a tattered old notebook. His desk was a disaster area. How could he find anything in the freaking mess of books and papers and who knew what else was hiding in there?

He was cute, in an absentminded kind of way. He kinda made her want to take care of him, like the lost puppies she used to try to bring home when she was a little girl.

Whoa! Take care of him? Roxy took a step away. What on earth was she thinking? Hadn't she had enough, taking care of Todd all those years? And for what? Years of empty promises followed by divorce papers.

This was *her* time. She was finally in control of her own life, finally getting the education she'd always wanted. She wasn't taking care of anyone but herself for at least the next four years.

While Dr. Jennings kept writing, Roxy wandered around the lab. In contrast to his desk, the rest of the room was immaculate. Spotless. Sterile, even. Test tubes of all sizes sat in racks along one counter and there were also a bunch of shiny equipment she couldn't even begin to name. Or imagine what they did. Long rows of intimidating lab tables filled the rest of the large room.

It was so quiet in here it was almost spooky. Roxy liked to

crank up music as loud as she could in order to concentrate. Hard rock that drove Gina crazy. Roxy liked to think the music forced all extraneous thoughts out of her mind when she was studying.

Gina said she thought Roxy didn't like the silence because it left her alone with her thoughts.

Roxy didn't want to think about that right now.

She was much more interested in looking at the attractive professor. He really was a hunk, with his strong jaw and chiseled features. His golden brown hair was thick and a little wavy. She was almost close enough to run her fingers through it before she caught herself.

What on earth? No way. She wasn't getting distracted by a good-looking guy. She hiked the strap of her book bag farther up her shoulder and put her hands behind her back before she actually reached out and touched him.

She didn't step away though. Instead, she looked over his shoulder again. Mmm, he smelled good. She couldn't make sense out of anything he wrote on the pages of the notebook. His scribblings looked like gibberish to her. "What'cha working on?"

He jumped to his feet, sending the chair rolling across the tile floor. Papers flew everywhere. He stared at her as if he had no clue why she was there. "Are you still here?"

"You offered me a ride home."

"Oh, right." There was that puppy dog look again, slightly confused yet intensely intelligent at the same time. "Um, can you give me a few minutes?"

She shrugged. "You know, I can walk home from here and you can keep doing whatever it is you're doing."

"No, I won't be long." He grabbed a battered briefcase from

underneath the desk and started cramming papers into it. He muttered to himself but Roxy couldn't make out any real words.

She knelt down and picked up the papers that had scattered on the floor. When she stood up to hand them to him, she found herself looking into his warm, dark eyes. Her heart kicked into high gear and her skin got all shivery. It was a long, hot moment before she could pull her gaze away.

He cleared his throat and added the papers to the rest in his briefcase. "Thank you." He latched it and set it down on the floor. "Let me get out of this."

Roxy watched as he unbuttoned the wrinkled white lab coat. When he stripped it from his body, she sucked in a deep breath. Whoa, the Doc was buff. How did a guy who spent all his time in a lab have a body like that? His legs were long and lean, encased in worn denim. His shirt covered a broad chest and flat abdomen. The shirttails were partially pulled out of the waistband of his jeans, making her heart pound just a little bit faster.

"You're not at all what I pictured when Gina talked about you," she said, needing words again to fill the charged silence.

He hung up the lab coat on a hook beside his desk and then turned around. A lopsided grin spread across his face. Oh, he was way too cute.

"Oh, really? How did you picture me?"

"Well, you're a lot younger than I thought you'd be."

He chuckled. "That's right. All college professors have thinning hair and bellies hanging over their belts."

Roxy let her gaze slowly travel over him, taking in again the long legs, the broad chest, the crooked grin. "Obviously not."

He cleared his throat and turned to grab his briefcase. "Ready to go?"

"Yeah."

The click of Roxy's heels echoed through the silent hallway. Dr. Jennings didn't say anything to her as they left the building, but she was picking up some sort of weird vibe she'd never felt before.

No, that wasn't true. She'd experienced something like it the first time she saw Todd Morgan and his killer dimples in ninth grade homeroom. It was almost like an electrical charge. Or a magnetic pull. It didn't have any logical explanation. It simply was.

Roxy stopped in her tracks. They were halfway across the parking lot, headed for some low-slung black sports car parked under a spotlight. The last thing she needed was a magnetic attraction to a man, any man, at this point in her life.

The autumn wind blew around her and she crossed her arms against the chill. She had all she could do to attend classes, work enough hours to pay the bills, and do all the homework that was overwhelming her. She did not need to get involved with a man.

Dr. Jennings must have finally noticed she no longer followed him. He turned around, his face in the shadows. "Did you forget something?"

She'd almost forgotten what was important. Control was. Education was. Magnetic pulls were not.

But he sure was good-looking. And nice. A gust of wind lifted her hair and blew its icy breath along her neck. She shivered. What harm was there in accepting a ride home after dark? It wasn't like they were going on a date or anything.

No dates until she had her degree.

"No, I'm okay." She caught up with him. To stop him from asking any other questions, she asked, "This your car?" Guys loved to talk about their cars. "Wow, a Porsche."

"Um, yeah." He opened the door for her, something Todd had never done for her in four years of high school and seven years of marriage. How had she let herself waste all those years of her life on a jerk?

She climbed in and tucked her long legs inside. Dr. Jennings closed the door, rounded the car, and climbed in beside her. He folded his legs under the steering wheel.

He turned to look at her. They were nearly nose to nose in the darkness of the vehicle. She could almost see the electrical charge sizzling between them. Her hands tingled. Her body buzzed. Oh, this was not good. Not good at all.

"Are you sure you're all right?" he asked, his voice soft.

"I'm fine, Dr. Jennings," she said. Shit, that sounded a little shaky. His musky scent seemed to fill her nostrils, flood her senses. "I...I have a lot of homework tonight."

"Then we better get you home," he said, starting the engine. He didn't pull out of the parking space right away. He turned and looked at her again, his face lit up by the spotlight. "You're not in any of my classes, are you?"

"Chemistry? No way."

"Good." There was that grin again. "Then you can call me Daniel."

Chapter Two

Roxy's laugh sounded a little shaky to Daniel. Was she nervous? Was she afraid of him? Could she actually be concerned about her safety? The wispy edges of her golden hair shimmered like a halo, but her face was in the shadows. Daniel knew that once he pulled out from under this light he wouldn't be able to see her at all.

And that would be a real shame.

She shifted in her seat. She glanced over at him through a veil of hair. The spotlight caught her face as she leaned forward and moistened her lips with the tip of her tongue. Then she brushed her hair back from her face and looked quickly away.

Insight struck Daniel like a sledge hammer. Attraction was a two-way street. Was it possible that Roxy was attracted to him as well? Was it possible the elixir worked both ways?

Of course. That's the way it should work. What good was a one-way attraction? How could he have neglected to take that into consideration? He needed to record more than just his own feelings and observations. He wasn't the only one involved. He would have to know Roxy's reactions also.

How did he do that without admitting the nature of his experiment? Certainly no woman would be pleased to know they were part of a study on the effects of a special pheromone-enhancing formula on sexual awareness. No woman would want to think she'd been manipulated. He'd have to try to work around it.

Small talk had never been his forte. Straightforward and to the point, that's the way he liked his conversations and his life. He took a deep breath and forced a smile.

Looking at Roxy, it was easier than he thought.

"Are you hungry?" he asked, hoping his voice sounded properly seductive.

She leaned forward again and looked at him through luscious lashes. "Hungry?"

That look caused him to think about an entirely different kind of hunger. "Um, for food?" He wanted to make that clear. To her. To himself. "I thought you might like to get something to eat before you dive into that homework."

"Oh." She plopped back against the seat and stared out the windshield. "I'm sorry, Dr. Jennings. I can't have dinner with you."

"Not dinner, just something to eat. And it's Daniel."

She wet her lips again. Daniel had to fight the urge to cover them with his own. He clutched the steering wheel with both hands so he wouldn't reach out and gather this perfect stranger into his arms.

He'd developed one heck of a love potion.

Correction, elixir. Attraction elixir.

Whatever he wanted to call it, it was working. And he had to find out how it worked on her.

"Come on, Roxy. I'm starved." Was he actually begging? "Don't make me eat burgers and fries by myself. I eat alone all the time."

Not that he minded. He actually preferred it that way. Really. But telling her that wouldn't get her into a neutral environment so he could interview her.

She sighed and glanced at him through her lashes again. "Okay. As long as it's something quick and cheap."

Daniel shifted into drive before she could change her mind. He pulled out of the parking lot and drove to a burger place not far from campus. It was filled with boisterous students and noisy young families. Perfect for what he needed. If it was too quiet, he imagined she would feel more uneasy being with him. And certainly not as forthcoming about the way she was feeling.

There was a table for two in the corner. Daniel almost grabbed her hand to lead her back there. He didn't think she'd appreciate it. He had to shove his hands into his pockets to keep from touching her. They skirted around a highchair and a spilled ice cube that skittered across the floor in front of them.

The table hadn't been cleared off yet from the previous customers. He watched as Roxy gathered up the plates, stacked them, placed the silverware on top and then collected the napkins and straw papers as well.

She caught him watching her. "Can't help it," she said with a shrug. "Occupational hazard."

"What do you mean?"

"I've waited tables since I was a kid," she told him. She cocked her head toward the busy waitress who was picking up the wayward ice cube before someone slipped on it. "I know what she's going through."

Daniel nodded as his mind scrambled for the best way to start the interview. How should he bring up the subject of sexual attraction to a woman he'd only met a few minutes ago? It would be awkward, but what kind of scientist would he be if he let an opportunity to gain information slip by?

Science was the search for knowledge. Knowledge was paramount. He'd heard that since he was a kid.

The waitress made her way to their table. She smiled her thanks for the stacked dishes. After she cleared them off, she came back with a rag to wipe off the table. Then she pulled a pen from behind her ear and pulled an order pad from the pocket of her apron. “Okay, now, what can I get you?”

“We’d like separate checks,” Roxy said quickly.

“No, Roxy. It’s my treat. My idea.”

She put her hand on his arm to silence him. Then she smiled at the waitress and said, “Separate checks.”

“Okay.” She took their orders and promised their soft drinks in a minute.

Roxy didn’t move her hand after the waitress left. He didn’t know whether it was on purpose or because she didn’t even think about it being there. Whatever the reason, it felt warm and soft against his skin.

Roxy didn’t look at him. She stared out the window at the headlights of the cars driving by. She was probably wondering why he practically dragged her here.

If he hadn’t slapped that elixir on tonight, would he have experienced anything at all when Roxy entered the lab? Would he have experienced a lesser attraction to her? Was it even possible that all his reactions tonight had nothing to do with his formula?

Impossible.

It was time to find out what he could about the other side of the attraction. How did his new elixir affect the other person?

He wished he’d brought his notebook in with him. He cleared his throat. “Roxy, can I ask you something?”

She looked over at him. He noticed her eyes were bright green. “Sure.”

“Are you attracted to me?”

Well, that sure wasn't what Roxy expected. Talk about direct and to the point. She realized her hand was still on Dr. Jennings' arm and she snatched it away. Her face heated beneath his gaze.

Her gift of gab had always been her saving grace. As a waitress in a busy restaurant, she'd heard every come-on and smart remark to come out of a guy's mouth. She was always ready with a quick comeback. So why was she tongue-tied when it came to Dr. Daniel Jennings?

Could it be because she absolutely was attracted to him? She wasn't sure she was ready to admit it to herself, much less to him. She didn't want to be attracted to him, or anybody else, at this point in her life.

He continued to study her, patiently waiting for her answer. His hazel eyes had flecks of brown and green, whirling together in an amazing pattern.

"I've never seen eyes like yours before." Duh, what a dumb thing to say. Why not just fall at his feet and gush something about getting lost in his gaze.

"So you find yourself attracted to my eyes?" he asked her. He didn't smile like he was amused by her comment. He appeared to be taking what she said very seriously.

"No. I mean, yes, but—" Roxy decided she might as well go for it. If he wanted straight and to the point, she could give it to him. Sort of. Her face grew warm but she pushed on. "I mean, any woman would think you were very attractive, Dr. Jennings. It's just that I..."

He shook his head. "It's Daniel. And no, most women don't seem to."

Yeah, right. "Then they're blind."

He smiled then. “So when was it that you first experienced the attraction, Roxy?”

They’d known each other less than an hour and he wanted her to pinpoint the moment of attraction? These scientist types really got off on this research stuff. “Man, Dr. Jennings...”

He placed his hand over hers and Fourth of July fireworks started exploding through her body.

“It’s Daniel.”

She pulled her hand out from under his and placed it in her lap. It shook just the slightest bit. “Okay.” She swallowed. “Daniel.” The waitress came with their drinks then. Roxy dragged her gaze away from Daniel and smiled at the waitress. “Thanks.” She sucked down half a glass of cola while she tried to think of a response.

“Roxy? Do I make you uncomfortable? Because that’s the last thing I want to do.”

He had the most sincere expression on his face. She’d have blown off anyone else who asked her a question like that, but with Daniel...what was it with Daniel?

“What is this, huh? Because I have to tell you, this is the strangest conversation I’ve ever had. And I’ve had my share.”

He folded his hands and placed them on the table in front of him. He had long, slender fingers. She really didn’t want to know how they’d feel on her bare skin, but a wave of light tingles danced along her arms just the same.

“I’d just like you to take a moment before our food arrives and think about when you first noticed you were attracted to me.”

“Look, Daniel, I want to get something out of the way right now. I’m not sure what you expected by taking me out for a burger, but I am not interested in dating.”

He frowned. "I thought we'd agreed this wasn't a date."

"Yeah, but with all these questions, I was afraid maybe you thought whatever this was could lead to a future date, and I wanted you to know it isn't going to happen."

He nodded in a resigned sort of way. "I get a lot of that. I know I'm not the most exciting guy. I don't play football. I don't mountain climb."

"No, no, it's nothing against you, I don't mountain climb either. And yes, I am attracted to you. But I have enough on my plate right now, Daniel. I don't have time for a relationship."

His face lit up and Roxy got a little boost knowing she'd done that. "But you are attracted to me. I knew it. When did you first notice the attraction, Roxy?"

"What is this? Some kind of survey? Shouldn't the psych department be doing research on the attraction habits of college students? I wouldn't think that would be the chemistry department."

"Don't they call a strong attraction between two people chemistry?"

She had to laugh. This was the most bizarre conversation she'd ever had, and he was so dead serious.

He joined her in the laughter. "Yes, okay, you got me. I'm helping out the psychology department. I was supposed to be a lot smoother in my questioning. Somehow, I couldn't think of a charming way to say, oh by the way, I need to know when you crossed the line between perfect stranger and interested perfect stranger."

Rosy laughed again. "Okay, Doc, I'll go along with you." She took a deep breath. Why did it suddenly feel as if she was spilling her guts? "Honestly? Right away. Like when I first saw you. You were staring at me like you'd seen a ghost and, suddenly, I just felt this magnetic pull."

Daniel grabbed a napkin out of the metal holder on the table and searched his pockets. “Magnetic pull. That’s good. Great. Where’s my pen?”

Roxy pulled a pen out of her bag and handed it to him. “I don’t know how good that pull really is.”

Daniel looked up from the words he was scrawling across the napkin. “Why not?”

How could he say he wasn’t exciting? The spark in his eyes was contagious. He probably lived for those words. Why not? Why? He was the kind of person who needed to know things. The energy around him was incredible and Roxy just sat there and tried to soak it up.

“I can’t believe you don’t have women falling all over you,” she said, rather than answer his question.

He started writing again. “Believe me, that’s not the case.”

“You’ve never been married?”

“I lived with a woman once...” His voice faded and he glanced up from the napkin and stared out the window.

After he was quiet for a whole thirty seconds, Roxy couldn’t stand it any longer. “What happened?”

He shrugged. “We were too much alike. Cynthia was a researcher, psychology as a matter of fact. We both stayed in our separate rooms with our separate studies and one day realized we were living in the same apartment but we never saw each other.”

He looked back to Roxy, his expression a bit sad. “When she left, I didn’t even miss her. My life didn’t change at all.”

“Really?” When Todd left, her whole world changed. No one to make snide comments about her weight. No one to hold dinner for and then eat alone, half the time anyway. No one to warm her bed at night. “Wait a minute. You didn’t miss the sex?"

What do you know, the Doc blushed. And almost choked on the soda he was drinking. "Well, sure," he said after a moment. "But not as much as I thought. That was part of the problem."

"Oh?"

He nodded. "I wouldn't even consider trying another relationship without the one thing that was lacking with Cynthia."

"What was that?"

"Passion."

Roxy thought she saw passion in his eyes right now. Boy, it really sucked she wasn't dating. She'd like to take him up on his search for passion. It wasn't too hard to imagine his strong hands on her body. His lips on her heated skin. His—

Damn it. Her timing had always been lousy.

Just because she wasn't dating, didn't mean he shouldn't. She took a deep breath. "Well, you're never going to find any passion if you stay locked away in your lab 'til all hours of the night."

He stuffed the napkin in his pocket and handed her the pen. "I wouldn't even know where to begin. I'm thirty-two years old. I should probably have 'confirmed bachelor' stamped across my forehead."

"That's crazy. There's lots of women out there. You have to know where to look, that's all. And how to dress..."

He spread his arms out wide. "What's wrong with how I dress?"

"Nothing." She lifted an eyebrow and pointed to his shirt. "What do you call that color anyway? Split-pea green? I know you're not dressed for a date right now, but that's the ugliest shirt I've ever seen. Are all of your clothes like these?"

He frowned. "What's wrong with blue jeans and button-down shirts?"

"You need a little variety, for starts. And some new colors. I could help you with that, you know. And you need to get out away from campus sometime. I mean, you're not in the market for a student, right? You want a woman with some experience."

"Experience?"

"Yeah, with passion. That's what you want, right? Passion?"

Daniel nodded. His eyes seemed to darken as he looked at her. Her stomach did a little flip.

"That's what I want," he replied.

"Well, Doc. I'll tell you what. I'm willing to help you in your search for a passionate woman."

He raised an eyebrow. "Oh? Why would you want to do that?"

Good question. Why on earth was she saying all this? Hadn't she just finished telling herself that the very last thing she needed was to get involved with another man? She didn't have time for this.

Roxy looked at Daniel and knew it was the pull. The attraction he'd been asking her about. It wouldn't let her go. She couldn't let him go, not yet. If she couldn't date him, she wanted another way to be around him just a little more.

"I've always been up for a challenge, Doc."

Chapter Three

She'd played right into his hands. Daniel couldn't believe it. Not that he needed help finding a woman. He could find one if he wanted to. Really. He was simply too busy with his work to play the dating game.

But now that the experiment had started, he had to continue his contact with Roxy. For better or worse, she was his research subject. The fact that she felt an immediate attraction to him as well was exciting news. It meant he was on the right track with his formula.

Their food came then and Daniel watched with interest as Roxy interacted with their waitress. She made eye contact and talked to her about the weather and asked if her feet were sore. They shared opinions about the best shoes for being on their feet for hours on end, and the waitress left their table with a wider smile on her face.

"Amazing," Daniel said.

Roxy looked up from her plate, ketchup bottle in her hand. "What?"

"I just realized I don't normally pay much attention to waiters and waitresses. You, however, treated her like a good friend."

"Waitresses are people too, you know," she said, waving the ketchup bottle at him. "We work hard. We have good days and bad days and deserve as much respect as anyone else."

"You're absolutely right. I will never look at waitresses the same again." Or look at Roxy the same way either.

He watched her bite into her hamburger with gusto. He had the feeling she would do everything with enthusiasm. Eating. Waitressing. Schoolwork. Kissing. Sex.

He probably should have gone directly home and taken a shower. He still had the elixir on his skin.

As it was, he couldn't look at Roxy without noticing the shimmer in her blonde hair, or the sparkle in her green eyes. The ribbed sweater she wore hugged her beautiful curves in ways that made his palms itch. She licked a little bit of ketchup off her lips with her tongue and his mouth went dry.

He had to get his mind off lips and tongues and sex. "So, Roxy, are you a grad student here?"

She shook her head. "No, I'm a lowly freshman."

"Really? You wanted to work for a few years before going back to school?"

"Something like that." She glanced out the window. "It's a long story I really don't want to get into tonight."

"Okay," he replied. "What's your major?"

"Communications." She placed the half-eaten burger down on her plate and began to gesture with her hands. "I'm going to be a DJ. I mean, getting paid for talking and playing music? How cool is that?" She grinned. "I'm learning there's a lot more to it than that, but I know it's something I would really enjoy doing."

Looking at Roxy, Daniel knew what he'd enjoy doing. First he'd plunge his hands into her silky hair. Then he'd taste her slick lips. Cup her full breasts in his hands and gently squeeze them.

Daniel pulled out the folded napkin he'd shoved into his pocket. "Could I borrow your pen again?"

"Uh, sure."

Uncharacteristic thoughts again. If he didn't know better, Daniel would say he was feeling passionate toward Roxy Morgan. His formula had been designed to simply heighten attraction, to give the body's natural pheromones a little boost. He hadn't expected powerful sexual desire to be such a strong side effect. It appeared his potion was performing much better than he expected.

"Um, Doc. We need to talk a little bit about your conversation skills."

He looked up from his notes. "What?"

"When you're having dinner with someone, you're supposed pay attention to them. Carry on a conversation. Not get lost in your own little world and write on napkins." She leaned across the table to get a look and her breasts spilled over onto the table top. Her breasts again. He was fixated on her breasts.

"What'cha writing?"

He tore his gaze away from her curves and looked back down at the white napkin now covered with black notes. "Something you said triggered some ideas for my research and I had to write my thoughts down before I forgot them. It's a curse of the scientist, I'm afraid."

"Yeah, well, explain that to the woman you're hoping to find passion with. Let me tell you, being ignored is at the top of the list of ways to guarantee you'll be going home by yourself."

"Right. I'll remember that." He shoved the napkin back into his pocket and handed her back her pen. "Thank you. I promise not to borrow it again."

"Oh, well, it's okay, because we both know we're going

home alone tonight." She winked at him and Daniel could only think of what a shame that was. "I wanted you to be aware of it, in case this was your normal activity when having dinner with a woman."

He grinned and finished the last of his fries. "Your comments are duly noted."

"So did you always want to be a chemistry professor?"

"Science runs in the family, you could say. My parents are both research scientists. They work for a large pharmaceutical company in Philadelphia." And had made it abundantly clear that, as far as they were concerned, his work wasn't important at all. Their life's ambition seemed to be to try to convince him to come to work with them.

"But how did you know you wanted to teach?" She picked up her hamburger again. "How did you know it was chemistry out of all the subjects out there?"

"Science was always easy for me," he went on, pushing his parents out of his mind, "but chemistry was exciting. It *is* exciting. I can't think of anything better than sharing that excitement with students, and helping them embrace all the possibilities science has to offer. That makes my job fun."

"That's what I want," Roxy said, her eyes lighting up. "I don't mean chemistry," she added with a laugh. "I want to be excited to go to work. I want to enjoy what I'm doing every day." She looked like she was about to say more, but she drained her cola and placed her napkin on the empty plate in front of her. "Now, I really have to get home and hit the books. I forgot how much time homework takes."

"Thank you for taking the time to answer my questions and saving me from eating another meal alone."

She smiled and if he'd had his pen with him he would have made note of how an odd sense of happiness washed over him at the small gesture.

"See," she said, "when you say things like that, Doc, I think you have a real chance of finding the woman you need."

Dr. Jennings dropped Roxy off at her apartment after they ate. It was easier to think of him as "Dr. Jennings" or "Doc" instead of "Daniel". Dr. Jennings, the Doc, was a college professor, super intelligent and way out of her league. Daniel was funny and sexy and could be a real distraction to her studies.

She couldn't believe she made plans to meet him tomorrow after school, instead of getting her homework done before she worked all weekend. See, he was already a distraction.

He was really taking this love lessons stuff seriously. Probably lonely, poor guy, if what Gina told her was true. Roxy was sure she'd have no trouble helping him get over the bumps of building a new relationship.

Not that she'd had any personal experience in the past few years. She'd had lots of opportunities—guys liked to flirt with her and she had no problem with a little harmless flirting right back. But Roxy believed in being faithful and keeping promises. Too bad her husband hadn't felt the same way.

She walked into the living room and tossed her keys onto the end table. When she switched on the classic rock station, she paused a moment to picture herself sitting at the controls, sending Bon Jovi out to all her listeners, keeping them awake with "Livin' on a Prayer" while they worked the swing shift or took a drive or dove into their homework.

Roxy dropped onto the sofa, careful to miss the renegade spring that threatened to goose her every chance it got. She dumped her books and notebooks on the coffee table. She had a dozen algebra problems, two chapters in history to read, and an essay to start for public speaking.

With any luck Gina would be gone all evening and Roxy could get her work done before her roommate came in and started talking.

She was so lucky to have found Gina when she advertised for a roommate after Todd left. While they seemed to be opposites in a lot of ways, they'd become great friends. When they were in the mood, Roxy and Gina could kick back and get a real gab-fest going. But homework was a lot harder than she remembered. She hoped she would have the apartment to herself tonight.

The Stones rocked out in the background as Roxy grabbed her algebra book. Might as well get the worst of it out of the way first. She was half-way through her math problems when the phone rang.

Roxy sighed and reached for the receiver. "Hello?"

"Roxy, thank God, you're home."

She could hear the muffled voices of the diner crowd in the background. That sound, and the clinking of the dishes, the rattle of silverware, had been the background music of her life while she was growing up. "Hi, Mom. What's wrong?"

"Amy's sick. I need you to come in."

Oh, man. Why did she answer the phone? She should have let the machine get it. "Mom, I can't come in. I have tons of homework to do tonight."

"It's wing night. The place is packed. I need you here."

Roxy looked at the piles of books and papers in front of her and cringed. "Call somebody else. I can't come in tonight."

"Everybody else worked all day so Little Miss Somebody could take college classes that won't do her an ounce of good in the real world."

Roxy clenched her teeth together so she wouldn't explode with the words that threatened to bust out of her. They had this conversation all the time. Roxy was tired of defending her choices. Her needs. Her mother had never understood.

The crash of breaking china shattered the tense silence. "Watch it!" her mother called. "Roxy, I gotta go. Get your butt down here right now."

The click was loud in Roxy's ear. Her stomach clenched in frustration and her head began to pound. She'd worked in that damn diner since she was old enough to hold a wet rag. She'd gone to school smelling like grease, and washed dishes or waited tables instead of participating in after-school activities. Her mother loved the restaurant and had made it her whole life.

Roxy wanted more.

She sighed deeply and rubbed her temples. She shouldn't have had dinner with Daniel, no matter what kind of pull she felt for him. No matter how much she yearned to touch him. Or wondered what his kiss would taste like.

She could have put a good dent in her studies by now if she'd come right home. Instead, she'd be up until the middle of the night to get it all done.

She stood and dragged herself into the bedroom to change into her waitress uniform.

"So when are you going to put Charlie out of his misery?" Roxy stood beside her mother in the doorway of the kitchen after the crowd had finally thinned out. Her head and eyes and feet were all killing her. She tried not to think about all the homework waiting for her when she got home.

"What are you talking about?" Her mother's cheeks looked a little flushed.

"Don't even pretend you don't know." Roxy nodded her head to the end of the counter. Charlie sat there eating his usual cheeseburger and fries. She worried about him sometimes. His cholesterol levels had to be through the roof.

Sandra Erickson glanced his way. "He doesn't look miserable to me." She turned abruptly and disappeared into the kitchen.

Roxy limped through the swinging door after her. "I think he's getting tired of waiting."

"Waiting for what? He got his dinner. That's what he came here for."

"That's not all he wants, and you know it."

"I don't need a man in my life."

Roxy could relate to that, but she couldn't help but feel sorry for Charlie. He was the closest thing she had to a father.

"I didn't tell him to keep hanging around here." Her mom grabbed a stack of dirty plates and dumped them into the sink. The crash was loud, but she was too much of a businesswoman to break any. "I told the man twenty years ago I didn't want to marry him. I told him the same thing twenty minutes ago. Why is he still hanging around?"

"Mom, you know why."

She turned the water on full blast and the spray soaked the front of her apron. "Roxy, I never mean-mouthed that father of yours, but he taught me years ago that men can't be trusted and I haven't seen anything since to change my mind."

Roxy could relate to that too.

Paulie Harrington, the dishwasher, just stood back in the corner behind her mother and watched her do his job.

She didn't look at Roxy, just squeezed some dishwashing liquid into the churning water. "Haven't I been doing all right? Didn't I keep a roof over your head and food in your stomach?"

"Of course, you did, but I haven't lived at home for a long time."

But she was on a roll and didn't seem to hear anything Roxy said. "And I didn't have to rely on a man for any of it."

"I know, Mom."

"And that man out there." She pointed at the door with a hand dripping with soapy water. "I don't need him. He's a nice man, but I don't need him, Roxy. I'll never need him."

"But don't you ever just want to be with a man?"

Her mother's eyes widened. "I don't care how old you are, little girl, I'm not about to discuss those things with you."

"I'm not talking just about sex, Mom." Although she couldn't imagine going all those years without sex. "What about companionship? What about conversation and laughter, don't you ever want that?"

"So was that man you married worth the heartache just for some conversation and laughs?" She shook her head. "I can get those here at the diner."

But not the sex. Roxy clamped her mouth shut before she said the words out loud.

"You're getting your wants and needs mixed up," Sandy went on. "I could have been selfish and thought of my own wants when I was raising you, but I didn't." She waved around a soapy dish before she plunged it into the rinse water. "And don't think I didn't have plenty of chances."

Roxy caught Paulie's eye behind her mom's back, and he raised his eyebrows and grinned.

"You were the most important thing in the world to me and

I didn't let anything get in the way of your needs." Her deep green eyes bore into Roxy. "Do you understand what I'm saying?"

Roxy grabbed the dish out of her mother's hand and gave it to Paulie to dry. She had to get out and check on her customers and refill coffee cups and pop glasses. "Yeah, I do. And believe me, I appreciate all you did for me when I was little. But, Mom, I'm all grown up now."

"Doesn't make any difference. I still worry about you. Make sure those fancy college classes you're taking are going to take care of your needs, Roxy."

"But I want to learn. What is so wrong with that?"

"Wants and needs, Roxy. Wants and needs."

"Smells like burnt toast in here."

Roxy watched Gina bop into the kitchen and frowned at her over her cup of chai tea. At least, she was pretty sure it was Gina. Roxy's vision was still a little blurry from staying up most of the night doing homework. Yep, it had to be Gina heading for the fruit bowl on the counter. No one else would wear those hideous red and purple paisley pajamas that almost swallowed her tiny frame.

"You look like hell."

"Oh, thank you very much," Roxy replied with a yawn. "You, on the other hand, look incredibly well-rested for someone who had a hot date last night."

Gina stopped peeling her banana in mid-peel. "How did you know I had a date last night? I never got a chance to tell you."

"Yeah. I hunted all over campus for you."

"Whoops. Sorry. Steve kinda took me by surprise. I forgot

you wanted a ride."

"Steve, huh? Cute Steve from the student union?"

"Yeah, but his personality wasn't as great as his looks." Gina shrugged. "Talk about boring. I thought I was going to fall asleep before we even got our food. Sorry again about leaving you hanging."

"No harm done. Doc gave me a ride home." Roxy picked the crust off her burnt toast and hoped she sounded nonchalant. "He's the one who told me about your date. So, tell me all the sordid details."

"What Doc?" Leave it to Gina to pick up on that one word. "Who the hell is Doc?"

"Doc. You know, Dr. Jennings." She avoided Gina's eyes and stared at the mess of toast crumbs she'd made in front of her. "Daniel?"

"Daniel?" Gina dropped her banana onto the counter and plopped down in the chair across the table from Roxy. "How on earth did you get on a first-name basis with my chemistry professor?"

"I told you. I went up to the chem lab looking for you. He gave me a ride home. Oh, and we stopped and had something to eat. I had to stay up 'til all hours getting my homework done."

"You had a date with Dr. Jennings?" Gina practically bounced in her chair. "Oh, my God! I think there's like a pool going on to guess when he'd actually go out with a woman. Some of the students think he's gay."

"It wasn't a date," Roxy said quickly. No dates until she got her degree. She had to keep repeating that before she let herself get distracted.

But she couldn't forget the heated looks Daniel gave her last night. Her body tingled just from the memory. "And he's definitely not gay. He had a long-term relationship with a psychologist that ended badly and he hasn't found anyone since who he feels passionate about."

"Oh, my God. You found out more in one night than I've learned after working with him for two years." Gina jumped up and grabbed the banana she'd left on the counter. "He's such a nice guy. I'd like to see him hook up with someone. But, well, he's never going to find a woman working the hours he does."

Roxy nodded. "That's what I told him. So I offered to help him."

Gina's dark brown eyes grew so big they almost took up her entire face. "You're going to get passionate with Dr. Jennings?"

Images of Daniel's hands on her body, Daniel's mouth on her skin warmed her all over. Roxy shook her head to get those fantasies out of her brain. "No. I'm going to help him find someone."

"Come on, Roxy, I think you guys would be good together. You haven't had a date since your divorce. You deserve a little passion too."

The tingles were working overtime. She had to think about something else. "No dates. I can't afford any passion right now. I have to concentrate on my schoolwork."

"I don't get it. What are you doing with Dr. Jennings then?"

"I'm just helping the guy out. You know, like a friend. I'm meeting him after classes tonight and we're going to go out."

"Ah ha! You are going out!"

"Not on a date!" Roxy wished she'd never mentioned it. "I'm just getting him out of his lab at a decent hour. Didn't we just agree that's what he had to do if he was going to find someone?"

Gina had such a skeptical look on her face. "What are you going to do on this non-date?"

"I'm taking him to the mall."

"Shopping? You're taking Dr. Jennings shopping?"

Roxy thought about the worn jeans that hugged his lean thighs. The ugly shirt that covered his broad chest. "He needs a little help in the clothing department. Dress that guy up right and he'll be fighting off women."

Gina shook her head. "I don't know. For someone who doesn't want to get involved with a man, you sound pretty involved already."

No way was Roxy telling Gina about the magnetic pull or the fireworks. "I'm just helping the guy out."

Chapter Four

Anticipation was a strange thing. Thoughts of Roxy curled though Daniel's brain all day long. He found it difficult to concentrate during his labs and lectures. Instead of his mind being on formulas and compounds, he couldn't stop thinking about red lips, tight sweaters and spontaneous laughter.

He debated how much of the elixir to use today. He thought it might be a good idea to use a lesser amount than he had the previous night. The problem was he had no idea how much he had used the first time.

He needed to know if the level of attraction would go up or down dependent upon the amount of elixir he used. Determining dosage would be an important step in developing and marketing his formula. He finally decided on an appropriate amount and then had to practically force Gina to leave before Roxy was due to show up.

As his lab assistant, Gina had been working on the formula with him, but Daniel was reluctant to tell her that he had started his experiment. For one thing, her roommate was the subject, so she might have a problem being unbiased. For another, he already knew what a big mouth Gina had. She'd never be able to keep from telling Roxy, and it would render all the data useless if Roxy was aware he was using her as part of the experiment.

A small twinge of guilt twisted in his stomach. Daniel liked Roxy. He regretted manipulating her emotions this way. But it wasn't anything he wasn't doing to himself too. And he was doing it in the name of science. His parents had taught him years ago that the search for knowledge was the most important thing in life. Nothing else mattered as much.

Not holidays. Not birthdays. Not graduations.

No wonder he had a problem with emotions. He'd probably never find a woman with whom he would be able to have a long-term relationship. He didn't even know what love was, much less how to fall in love with a woman he'd want to share his life with.

He wasn't willing to settle for the sterile marriage his parents had. He didn't want to raise children in a loveless home, where research books and studies were more important than hugs and kisses. But he wasn't sure he knew any other way.

What was he doing getting involved with a woman like Roxy? Someone who was so obviously full of life and enthusiasm? She wasn't the type of person who needed an attraction elixir to find a man. All she had to do was smile and say hello. Who could resist her?

Or was that the elixir talking? Daniel frowned as he rubbed the formula along his chin and jaw. How could he know if any of his reactions to Roxy were due to the potion, or if it was perhaps a heightened response because of it?

He heard footsteps coming down the hall. His heart started to race. His palms immediately began to sweat. He forced himself to stay beside his desk instead of dashing to the doorway to watch her approach.

Then, finally, she was there. His pulse skipped as he stared at her. Her shiny blonde hair stood out against a long black sweater she wore over a white blouse with a deep V-neck and a long black skirt and boots. She seemed to hesitate before stepping from the hallway into the lab.

He took a step forward. He didn't care how eager he looked. It was out of his control. "Hello."

She smiled then and walked into the room. "Hi."

"How were your classes today?" He was so lousy at small talk.

"Okay. But tell me something, Doc. Why do professors always pile on the homework over the weekend?"

Was this a trick question? "Because you have all weekend to do it?"

"I think it's because you want to ruin our Friday nights," she replied. The look on her face told him she wasn't joking.

He took another step closer. It took all his effort not to close the space between them and take her into his arms. "I certainly don't want to ruin your Friday night, Roxy."

She slowly crossed the room, her hips swaying with each step. With the high heels on her boots, she was nearly as tall as he was. "Good. I could really use a fun Friday night."

"Would you rather do something other than shopping?"

"What? You don't think shopping is fun?" she asked with a raise of her eyebrows. "Don't worry. We'll hit the mall and I'll get my second wind." She dragged her gaze slowly up his body. He could feel each spot where her eyes lingered. Legs. Crotch. Abs. Pecs. Lips. "Did you get those ugly shirts on sale?"

"I don't remember where I got them." He indulged in his own sweep of her body. Legs. Hips. Waist. Breasts. Lips.

Very nice. Was his mouth starting to water?

"Well, we have to get you some new shirts. Do you have any pants other than threadbare jeans?"

"A few." He didn't want to tell her he had a closet full of clothing. Cynthia had insisted he have appropriate clothing for the times she wanted to go out. He was interested to see what kind of clothes Roxy would pick out for him.

Then he'd have to wonder if her choices would have been different if not for the elixir.

"You need a couple pair of casual pants, like khakis. Some new jeans. Then at least one pair of dress pants for when you want to treat your new woman to a night on the town."

"Whatever you say." Right now he couldn't think of any other woman besides Roxy. He couldn't remember any eyes as bright and beautiful as hers. Or any body he wanted to touch more than hers. Her scent drifted around him, making him feel a little off center. Maybe he still put on too much of the potion.

"Then let's go."

She took his hand in hers as if it was the most natural thing in the world. Daniel swore an actual crackle shot up his arm. He grabbed his coat with his other hand and walked beside her out the door.

"Wow, this is a nice shirt." Roxy fingered the dove gray shirt that would go perfectly with the black trousers they'd already picked out. The fabric was so soft and smooth. She glanced at the price tag. Whoa. She'd never spent that much for an entire outfit. Or two. She started to steer Daniel away. "Never mind. Let's check these over here."

Daniel stopped in front of the row of obscenely expensive shirts. "What? Do you like this one?"

"Yeah, it's great, but it costs way too much."

Daniel looked at the price tag and shrugged. "If you like it, that's all I care about."

"But the price."

He reached for the shirt. "It doesn't matter."

"But it's so expensive."

"It doesn't matter," he repeated. He walked into a nearby dressing room, but left the curtain open.

Roxy had never known a time when the price didn't matter to her. Then she remembered the Porsche with the soft leather seats. "Okay. I guess college professors make a lot more than I thought they did."

Daniel chuckled and began to unbutton his ugly brown shirt. "Actually, I do some research on my own time and some of it has been...um...profitable. I've developed a couple products that have sold rather well."

He stripped the shirt from his body. The amazing fact that he'd gotten rich from his own inventions had only a second to register before it flew right out of her head. The breath left her body in a big whoosh. She stared at muscled pecs and washboard abs.

Whoa. The Doc definitely worked out.

A light dusting of hair swirled around on his chest between his nipples, then swept lower across his abdomen before disappearing below the waistband of his jeans. When she realized where she was looking, Roxy shot her gaze back up to Daniel's face.

The amused smirk on his face did more than irritate her. It made her want to cover his lips with hers, made her want to shock him into feeling the same kind of awareness that she did. Made her want his heart to pound just as hard and his skin to tingle just like hers did.

He winked at her.

Her face grew hot and she looked away. As she fumbled with the buttons on the gray shirt, she said as casually as possible, "So, what gym do you go to?"

He took the shirt from her and finished undoing the buttons. "I don't belong to a gym."

"Right. You just naturally have muscles like that from standing over test tubes all day."

He slid his arms into the sleeves and pulled the shirt on over his broad shoulders. Roxy couldn't stop herself from stepping up to him and buttoning the shirt.

"I have some workout equipment at home," he told her. He pushed back a lock of her hair that had fallen in her face and softly tucked it behind her ear. "It started as an experiment."

His hand lingered on her cheek and she couldn't resist leaning her face into his palm. "Um...experiment?"

She felt ridiculously disappointed when he dropped his hand. "For a protein supplement I developed. It allows me to get the benefits of a workout in much less time. I don't have a lot of time to work out."

She stepped back and looked him over again. "Well, I guess it worked."

"Yeah."

"So is this protein supplement one of the products you were talking about?"

He grinned. "Turns out there's a huge market for it."

"I'll bet."

She stepped forward again before she even realized it. Her eyes locked with his. She ran her hand down the front of the shirt, feeling his solid torso beneath her palm. Feeling the warmth of his body through the soft fabric. He took a deep breath and she felt his chest lift. Her mouth went instantly dry and she had to swallow before she could speak.

"I, uh, I really like this shirt." She pulled her hand away and gestured to the full-length mirror. "I think it looks good on you. What do you think?"

Daniel turned back to the mirror but she didn't think he even glanced at himself. He gazed at her reflection behind him in the mirror. "If you like it, I'll take it."

He turned around to face her and began unbuttoning the shirt. Roxy stepped back and curled her hands into fists to stop herself from touching him again. Then she winced from the pain when her fingernails dug into her palms.

She couldn't believe she'd touched him like that. What was she thinking?

She was not getting involved with another man right now. She mentally ran over the list of reasons. She deserved to have this time for herself after wasting so much time and energy on Todd. She deserved to focus her attention on her education without distractions.

And last but not least, if she didn't get her education, she'd never sit in that broadcast booth playing rock and roll. She'd never look forward to going to work every day. She'd be stuck working in Sandy's Diner for the rest of her life.

That was all the reminder she needed. She liked Daniel. She was going to help him find a woman to bring passion into his life. She was not going to be that woman.

Time to bring the conversation back where it belonged. "So, did you like the fit?"

"The fit?" He shrugged the shirt off.

He was bare-chested again. It took her a moment to remember what they were talking about. "The shirt. Did it fit okay?"

He shrugged and looked at the shirt in his hand. "I guess it was fine."

"Then, since you're on a spending spree, would you like a couple other colors too while we're here? Or do you want to check somewhere else?"

"If I get a couple more of these, will we be done shopping?"

"Yes, we'll be done."

His eyes brightened. "I'll take white and blue."

She couldn't think straight when he smiled like that. She turned away from him and grabbed the black trousers. "Okay, how about you wear that shirt with these black pants?"

"You mean change now?"

"Sure. They'll let you wear them out of the store. As long as you pay for them, of course."

He frowned. "Why do I have to change now? Where are we going?"

"There's this new place I've heard about over on Main Street. Good food and a great dance floor."

"Dancing?" He took a step back and bumped into the wall. "Oh, I don't know about that."

"Hey, I'll even throw in a dancing lesson," she told him, "but we don't have to dance if you don't want to." She hoped that he'd change his mind once they got there. The music was bound to be loud, just the way she liked it. And it would be a great excuse to feel his arms around her.

That was not the way her mind should be going. "I've heard it's always crowded. Should be a good place for you to meet some chicks."

"I'm not sure I'm ready to meet anybody yet." With his back to the changing room mirror, she had a great view of his mighty fine ass. Mouthwatering fine.

"Come on, Doc. When is anyone ever ready? But you've gotta start looking. The right woman's out there for you somewhere." She tried to keep her voice light and upbeat. "I'm hungry. Let's try it out."

He didn't look convinced, but he took the gray shirt and black pants and closed the curtain.

"If you need help," she called after him, "just let me know!"

"Are you sure this is the place?" Daniel paused in front of an ornately carved wooden door that said Le Club in red letters. Here on the sidewalk, the music was already louder than he liked.

Roxy nodded and slipped her hand in his. It felt more than right. It felt like it belonged. "This is the place."

He opened the door and she led them into the midst of chaos. Music blared from every direction. Lights flashed around them. The dance floor took up the entire lower level of the club. Bodies whirled and pulsed in all directions. A bar ran across one wall. There were tables on the second floor that ringed the dance floor.

His head started pounding immediately. If this was what he was missing by staying in his lab, he hadn't missed much. A tug on his arm brought his attention away from the whirling sea of people.

"Do you know how many decibels this noise would register?"

Roxy leaned close to him and pointed upstairs. "Come on, Doc. Don't get all scientific on me. Let's go find a table."

He nodded. If this was what she wanted, he'd give it a try, but he couldn't imagine meeting any women this way. Hopefully they wouldn't be here long enough to suffer any permanent hearing damage.

Suddenly, her face twisted in what appeared to be alarm. Or disgust. She shook her head and tugged him back toward the door. "Never mind. Let's get out of here."

"What's the matter?"

Before they could reach the door, a tall man with blond hair and broad shoulders stepped in front of them, blocking their way.

"Well, well, Roxy. What are you doing here?" His snide tone had Daniel bristling.

Daniel's hand was on the small of her back, and he could feel her stiffen. "This is a public place, Todd," she snapped. "I can be here if I want."

Todd's thin lips turned up into a smarmy smile. "Of course, you can. I just thought this place would be a little upscale for your taste."

"If I'd known this was where the fucking lawyers hang out, I never would have set foot in the door."

He sneered. "That trashy mouth is one of the reasons I left you."

Anger, red and hot, flared within Daniel. He stepped up and put his arm around her. It was either that, or give the jerk an upper cut to the jaw, and Daniel had never hit anyone before in his life. "Is there a problem, Roxy?"

She leaned into him. "This is my ex-husband, Todd Morgan. He's not a problem, he's just an asshole. Todd, this is Dr. Daniel Jennings."

Why did it surprise him so to find out she had been married? Maybe it was finding out she'd been married to a jerk. Or maybe it was wondering how anyone could have let her go.

"*Doctor* Jennings?" Morgan raised an eyebrow.

"That's right. I'm a professor at CSU."

"Someone told me you'd started college, Roxy. I told him he had to be joking. You and studying were never a good combination."

Roxy balled her hand into a fist at her side. Daniel grasped her hand and relaxed her fingers, threading them with his. He pressed against her and leaned close to her ear. "Let's get out of here."

"Todd?" A young woman, frighteningly thin, came up to them. Her flimsy dress showed off her total lack of curves. "I've been waiting for you at the bar."

"We were just leaving," Daniel said. His head pounded from more than the loud music. "Excuse us." He led Roxy around Morgan and out the door.

The relative quiet on the bustling sidewalk was a blessed relief. Cowden was a busy place on a Friday night. Roxy turned and put her arms around his waist and leaned against him.

He gathered her close. "Are you all right?"

She nodded, rubbing her cheek against his. "I'm just so ticked at myself. It's been over a year. Why do I let him get to me?" She stepped away from him and took a deep breath. And one more. "Okay. Seeing him is not going to ruin my evening. I'm still starving. Where can we go to eat?"

"I know a nice, quiet place," he told her, leading her back to his car. "You might call it boring, but they have excellent Italian food, play old classics, and have a tiny dance floor no one ever dances on."

"Sounds perfect." Roxy sank back against the leather seat and sighed. "Tell me about it."

"Well, I discovered Cala's a couple years ago," Daniel told

her as he started the engine and pulled out onto the street. "An old Italian couple runs it like you're in their home and they're serving family. I stop in about once a week."

"Mmm. Wonderful."

That magnetic pull Roxy had talked about last night was still at work. Daniel wanted nothing more than to stop the car and gather her into his arms. He could go without lasagna, but he didn't know how much longer he'd be able to go without a taste of her lips.

Her eyes were closed when he pulled up in front of the restaurant. Daniel took advantage of the moment to look at her in the glow of the streetlight. Had he only met her yesterday? Could one of the effects of his formula be a sense of belonging? A feeling that you've known the other person your whole life?

Her long lashes fluttered against her soft cheeks. At least, they appeared to be soft. Daniel couldn't resist finding out for certain. He reached out and stroked her face with one finger, gliding it along her perfect skin. He swept his finger from her temple, along her cheekbone, and down to her shiny red lips.

He drew his finger along her full lower lip and felt her smile. She opened her eyes.

"Are we there?"

"Yes. But if you're too tired, I understand. I can take you home."

"No way." She sat up. "I'm not tired. It was just awesome to relax for a few minutes." She opened the car door and stepped out onto the sidewalk. "I'm ready. Mmm, I can smell that sauce from here. My mouth is watering for spaghetti and meatballs."

"Then this is the place."

The restaurant wasn't very crowded when they walked in. A few other couples sat in booths along the far wall. The lights were dim as usual and Frank Sinatra crooned from speakers in the ceiling.

"Dr. Jennings." Mrs. Cala rushed over to the door, a large red apron covering her flowered dress. "So good to see you tonight."

"Hello, Mama," Daniel said and leaned over to kiss her cheek as had somehow become a custom. "I've been bragging to my friend, Roxy, about your delicious food and she insisted we come here for dinner."

Mrs. Cala swept Roxy into a big hug. "Welcome. Call me Mama. Come, you sit over here."

She set them at a tiny table for two next to a dance floor the size of a postage stamp. A red rose sat in a bud vase in the center of the table. The petals looked as soft as Roxy's skin.

"You want some wine?" Mrs. Cala asked. "I have a good Lambrusco all chilled and ready for you."

Daniel glanced with a questioning gaze to Roxy and she nodded. "That sounds perfect," he said. "Thank you."

Mrs. Cala nodded as well. "Good. Good. I'll be right back."

A melancholy love song drifted on the air by a singer he didn't recognize. A soft murmur of conversation buzzed around them. He tried to decipher the pensive expression on her face. Was that a look of longing, or was she simply as exhausted as he feared she was?

"Daniel?"

The sound of his name coming from her lips sounded better than it probably should have. No Doc this time. He was Daniel and her tone was wistful. He didn't want to remember that all this emotion was a product of his new formula. He didn't want to think about all the notes he'd have to make when he got back home tonight.

He didn't want to think of this night as part of an experiment. He foolishly wished it could be real.

Daniel? Had she actually breathed his name like a sigh? Roxy straightened her shoulders and sat up in the chair. She'd almost acted like this was a real date. She'd almost let herself feel like this attraction could go somewhere.

"Hey, Doc. How about we get that dance lesson out of the way?"

He frowned. Probably confused by her change of attitude. Who could blame him?

"All right."

Did he really sound disappointed?

"I'm afraid once I have a belly full of pasta, I won't want to get up on the dance floor."

Daniel held out his hand to her. "Miss Morgan, may I have this dance?"

She took his hand and let him pull her to her feet. "Um, yeah, but actually, I suppose it's technically Mrs. Morgan."

"You did say *ex*-husband, didn't you?"

She nodded. "I've been meaning to change back to my maiden name, but I just haven't gotten around to it. Though after tonight, I think I'm going to find the time."

Why on earth were they talking about Todd? The warmth of Daniel's hand on hers threatened to melt her into a puddle on the floor. The last thing she wanted to be thinking about was the ex-husband who had made her feel fat and unworthy.

This was her only chance to be in Daniel's arms. All she wanted to think about right now was Daniel and the dance.

They stepped onto the little square of wood and finally she was in Daniel's arms, right where she longed to be. Perry

Como—or maybe it was Tony Bennett—serenaded them.

She tried to be so strong all the time. To be in control. Was it so wrong to lean on someone else, just for the length of an old love song?

Roxy closed her eyes and pretended they were the only two people in the city at the moment. She could forget about ex-husbands, homework and daily specials, and concentrate on the mood and the music and the man. She felt safe and warm in his arms in a way she never remembered feeling before.

Pressed up against Daniel's hard body, the safe and warm feeling soon gave way to hot and dangerous sensations. They swayed to the music, their bodies rubbing, their thighs brushing, their breaths mingling.

His hands roamed over her back, stroking her, gathering her even closer to him. Her heart thudded in her chest, a frantic counter-rhythm to the soothing music surrounding them. Those tingles that danced in her body last night had taken flight and were now soaring through her veins.

She rubbed her cheek against his, the scraping of his jaw increasing the shocks of awareness running through her. She flattened her hands across his back and the heat radiating there warmed her to the center of her being.

Then his hands were in her hair, tangling in the strands, tickling her scalp. And, as if the sensations weren't already overwhelming, he started teasing her ear with his lips, nibbling gently. He brushed his hips against hers, his arousal clearly evident.

She pressed back.

Roxy bit back a moan. What was she doing? How quickly she'd forgotten all her good intentions. The last thing she needed was a man who made her lose control.

If nothing else, she had to stay in control.

The song was winding down. The rest of the world started to come back into focus. Roxy relaxed her grip and stepped away from Daniel. She shoved a shaky hand through her hair.

"Well," she said, grateful her voice didn't quiver like her knees were. "That was very good. I guess you don't need any dancing lessons."

Daniel cupped his hand around the back of her head and didn't let her retreat any further. The heat of his gaze pinned her as effectively as his hand did. Rosemary Clooney started singing and he pulled Roxy into his arms again. "I never said I needed dancing lessons."

His breath was warm on her neck and she sighed as she sank against him. "From what you said earlier, I thought you didn't dance."

"I don't usually like to," he said. He surprised her by spinning her out and bringing her back to tuck in against him. "I've changed my mind."

"Oh?" She told herself she was breathless from the whirling, but she knew that wasn't the reason.

"Mmm. I think dancing has become one of my favorite activities."

"I like to dance too." She rested her head on his shoulder and inhaled that unique Daniel scent again. Nice.

"So how long were you married?" he asked, so softly she almost didn't realize he'd spoken.

"Seven long years." She didn't want to think about Todd when she was in Daniel's arms, but since they were practically dirty dancing, she supposed he deserved to know. "I got married right out of high school. Pretty stupid."

"I imagine you thought you were in love."

"At the time I did. And Todd, well, he could be mighty

persuasive when he wanted to be. Besides...” Roxy broke off. She really didn’t need to go there.

He rubbed his cheek against hers. “What?”

“I wanted to get out from under my mom’s thumb.” Talk about being young and naïve. “Like getting married to Todd gave me any more control over my life.”

She cleared her throat. That was probably more than she needed to say to Daniel. “And then I worked full-time so he could go to college and then get his law degree. What can I say? I was young and stupid.”

Daniel’s grip tightened on her back. It was obvious he could do the math. “So he let you put him through school and then divorced you?”

The song wasn’t over, but she stepped away, out of his arms. “Yeah, that’s about the size of it.”

“Damn.”

Roxy took a deep breath and let it out slowly. She’d wasted all the anger she was going to on Todd Morgan. And she sure didn’t want Dr. Daniel Jennings feeling sorry for her. “Well, I’d say I’m more than ready for that wine. Let’s drink a toast to the ex who finally got away.”

The wine was excellent, the pasta was delicious, and the conversation was light for the rest of the evening. They discussed course options and campus activities. He was easy to talk to, even though he had earned a doctorate and she barely had her high school diploma.

Her resolve slipped and it made her more than a little nervous. Daniel was a nice man, but he was looking for a woman to settle down with and she wasn’t going there again for years. Her stomach clenched at the thought of another woman wrapped up in his arms, another woman dirty dancing with him, but that was the only way it could be right now. He was a distraction and she couldn't afford to be sidetracked right now.

Her next step was to find a good woman to give him the passion he'd been missing. It was a real shame it couldn't be her.

Roxy couldn't fall asleep no matter how tired she was. She tossed and turned after she got home, reliving dancing in Daniel's arms and putting up with Todd's snide comments. Would she ever be rid of Todd and the way he had of making her feel like a fool?

She'd been so clueless. She hadn't even minded working her ass off at the diner and then coming home to their little apartment and cooking and cleaning and taking care of every little thing so Todd could study to be a big, bad lawyer. She had been investing in their future. Her time would come.

Her time came all right. The night he passed the bar exam, he went out partying with a bunch of other newbie lawyers and called Roxy from whatever nightspot they were at to tell her he wanted a divorce. It probably took him at least three martinis to get up the nerve.

She'd just dragged herself in from the diner after pulling a double shift. With raucous laughter in the background, he complained that she was always tired, a lousy lover, and too fat to be a lawyer's wife.

She remembered slumping down onto the bed, too numb to cry, too exhausted to scream. The worst thing was that she never saw it coming. She'd believed every single one of those lies he fed her all those years. Did he ever really love her?

Did he mean it when he said he loved her back in high school, or was that just a way to get into her pants in the backseat of his old Chevy out on the old lake road? And what about when he asked her to marry him the summer after graduation? Did he know even then that he would need someone to pay all the bills while he went to college and law school? Someone dumb enough to work the treads off her sneakers while he went to classes and studied. Someone who tired herself out so much working a million hours a week that she wouldn't notice all the stories he made up about where he was and what he was doing and who he was doing it with.

If Roxy ever believed in love before that drunken telephone call, she'd never believed in it since.

It didn't take long that night for the numbness to wear off and the anger to set in. It was mostly anger at herself for her stupidity. At wasting all those years when she could have been doing something with her life. At putting her life on hold for a lousy lying son of a bitch.

Okay, so there was a lot of anger focused at Todd too.

She'd clenched the cordless phone in her hand long after Todd had hung up. When she started thinking about all the things she could have done since high school, she wanted to cry. Instead she screamed and threw pillows around the room and cursed a blue streak.

Suddenly she had a big burst of energy. He wanted her out of his life? Ha! She wanted him out of hers! She jumped to her feet and started yanking out dresser drawers. She never even noticed that Todd had more drawers full of clothes than she did. How did that happen?

She marched each drawer, one by one, to the door of their apartment, and then dumped them down the stairs toward the tiny landing at the bottom. Next went all the clothes from his side of the closet. And the pile of textbooks made lovely loud thuds as they bounced down the twelve steps, mixing up with the strewn jeans and button-down shirts and dry-clean-only suits.

In her anger, she forgot about the landlords. Mr. and Mrs. Campbell still lived on the first floor, a sweet old couple who'd always been pleasant but the not-butting-in type. As Todd's hundred-pound-apiece textbooks started bouncing down the stairs, Mr. Campbell stuck his bald head out the side door and just missed getting hit in the head. "Look out!" she cried.

"What's going on, Roxy?" he asked, rubbing his eyes. Poor guy. It was eleven o'clock at night and he'd probably been in bed for a couple hours already.

"Sorry, Mr. Campbell," she called down the stairs. "I didn't mean to wake you up. I'm just getting rid of some garbage."

Mrs. Campbell peeked out then, squinting through her thick glasses. "Throwing the bum out, are you?"

Roxy dropped the book she'd been holding and just missed smashing her foot. "What?"

"Sweetie, we always knew you were too good for him." She stepped out onto the landing in her nightgown. Roxy could still see her skinny white legs glowing in the light of the forty-watt light-bulb overhead. "Need some help?"

"No thanks, I'm almost done." She smiled for the first time since she discovered her life was one big mistake. "Oh, but would you mind if I changed the lock in the morning?"

"Don't you worry about a thing," Mr. Campbell said. "I think I have another one right here." He disappeared into his apartment for a moment, and then a few minutes later he slowly climbed the stairs in his plaid pajamas and slippers, a lock in one hand and a screwdriver in the other. "I don't want him bothering you tonight."

A lump caught in her throat as she remembered that night. Not because her husband didn't care about her. But because that dear old couple did.

Chapter Five

"Hey, Dr. Jennings, what's up?"

Daniel looked up from his desk to see Gina walking toward him. He took off his glasses and rubbed his eyes. He'd been working on his notes for what seemed like hours. No matter how he phrased it, he wasn't able to keep his personal feelings out of the equation. Personal feelings had no place in scientific research.

Just ask his parents.

Science was impersonal. Just because the experiment dealt with emotions didn't mean he couldn't be impartial. He had to find a way to record the facts and leave his feelings out of it.

"Is it four o'clock already?"

"Time flies," Gina replied. She sidled up to his desk and leaned her hip against it. "I can't believe you went out on a date with my roommate."

"It wasn't a date." Although he found himself wishing that it was. That was part of the problem. "She made that real clear."

"Yeah, yeah, Roxy keeps saying she won't date until she's gotten her degree. But you went shopping, and out to dinner and dancing. Sounds like a date to me."

"Well, it wasn't." Daniel closed his notebook. "Ready to work on the formula today?"

"Sure, but, um, Dr. Jennings? When are we going to try it out? I mean, how can we be sure it works until we actually pick a guinea pig and..."

"Guinea pig? Gina, haven't I taught you better than that?"

"Sorry." Her pretty face grew bright pink in an instant. "You know what I mean. Research subject. When are we going to try out the formula on a research subject?"

"Soon." Daniel knew he'd have to tell her what he was doing before too long. But not today. He handed her the folder of printouts. "I'd like you to go over the formula one more time and be on the lookout for any possible chemical reactions among the ingredients. We don't want all our work to be for nothing because of an adverse reaction to the skin tissue."

"Yeah, nothing worse than a skin rash to kill a romantic mood." Gina took the folder over to her desk.

Daniel opened his notebook again and tried to focus on his work. He tapped his pencil on the table. He had never had a problem like this before. Throwing himself into his work had always been the way for him to take his mind off anything else. His parents and their disappointment of his accomplishments, or lack thereof. Cynthia and their mutual disappointments of their relationship, or lack thereof. His loneliness.

But no amount of work seemed to take his mind off of Roxy.

"So, Gina, what did you and Roxy do all weekend?" Daniel couldn't believe the words had actually come out of his mouth. Just because he was thinking them, didn't mean they should have been said out loud.

Gina looked over at him with a grin. "Just curious, Professor?"

He cleared his throat. "Yes, that's right. Just curious."

"Well, I did homework and watched a lousy movie Saturday night. Roxy works double shifts Saturday and Sunday so she can go to school full time. Then she tries to fit in all that extra homework you professors like to dish out cuz, you know, you think we all have this extra time on the weekend."

Roxy had been exhausted when they went out to dinner, and it hadn't even been the weekend yet. "How does she manage it?"

"She doesn't get a whole lot of sleep," Gina said wryly.

He closed his notebook. He'd had enough of research notes for today. "Is she going to be home tonight?"

"Nope. She works Monday and Tuesday nights too."

He couldn't wait until Wednesday to see her again. "Where does she work?"

"Hey, Roxy, hon, can I have some more coffee?"

Roxy looked up from the textbook she had propped behind the counter. Charlie smiled at her through his scruffy beard from his usual stool. Mondays were typically slow and she hoped she'd get a chance to finish at least some of her homework between customers.

"Sure thing." She grabbed the coffee pot, walked down to the end of the counter and quickly refilled his cup. "New haircut, Charlie? You look especially fine tonight."

"Same old haircut, but thanks anyway, hon."

Cowden sat on the edge of Lake Erie, a mixture of college town and factory town. Her mother's generation was pretty much all blue collar, factory and service workers content to spend the rest of their lives here in town. Most of their children were going to college to try to get out.

It wasn't easy trying to plan to escape what your life had become when your life was so busy you couldn't think about anything else but getting through from the alarm clock ringing in the morning until you collapsed into bed at night.

So she kept waiting tables while she tried to decide what she really wanted to be when she grew up. Then, one night a few months ago, she couldn't sleep, despite how exhausted she'd been. Restless and edgy, she'd known if she didn't make a decision soon, she'd wake up one morning forty-five years old and still working at the diner. She'd switched on the radio and turned it up loud while she paced her bedroom.

The late-night DJ was a woman who played some of Roxy's classic rock favorites and chatted about making dreams come true, inviting listeners to call in and share their inspiring stories. But it wasn't the motivational stories that started Roxy's heart beating faster. It was the DJ, whose voice seemed to be speaking right at her. It was the DJ, playing the kind of music that stirred Roxy's blood and her imagination. And she knew without a doubt what she wanted to do with the rest of her life.

The next morning, Roxy checked with CSU and discovered they offered a communications degree and she hadn't looked back since. She hadn't had time anyway.

She made a quick sweep of the dining room, a pot of regular coffee in one hand, decaf in the other. Most of the people here tonight were regulars. People she had known for most of her life.

Amy, the other waitress on, was supposed to be on a quick break, but Roxy had already taken orders for more than a couple of her tables and checked out a couple more. She wished Amy would get her butt back out there. Her feet were killing her and she wanted to finish her chapter.

She was refilling Mrs. Perry's coffee cup when she heard the front door open. Her heart started pounding before she even saw Daniel walk through the door. She almost spilled the coffee, but she was too experienced a waitress to do that, even when distracted by the sexiest man she'd ever met.

He stood in the doorway and watched her. He wore a black leather jacket over the new white shirt he'd tucked into his old blue jeans. A shiver of awareness ran through her. What was he doing here? Didn't he live in his lab?

"Roxy!" Her name came over the loud speaker. Another one of her orders was up. She walked up to Daniel on her way to the kitchen.

She pasted her best waitress smile on her face. "Hey, Doc. What'cha doing here?"

The intense look on his face let her know exactly why he was here. "I'm hungry."

"Then you've come to the right place," she said, annoyed that her voice was actually a little shaky. She'd been hoping for perky. "Sit anywhere you want and someone will be right with you."

He placed a hand on her arm and she almost dropped the coffee pot. "Which section is yours?"

Right now the whole damn restaurant. "You can grab an empty stool at the counter."

"Roxy!" Her mother's voice over the speaker was more insistent.

"I have to get that," she said.

He nodded and dropped his hand.

She turned and set the coffee pots back on the warmers and fled to the kitchen. Plates and food were flying. Ralph, the cook, was broiling steaks, flipping burgers and heating up entrees. Paulie rattled china and silverware. Her mother was dishing up salads.

"What took you so long?"

Roxy picked up the plates for table four. "Where the hell is Amy? I can't take care of the whole restaurant by myself."

"She ran home to check on Scott real quick. He wasn't feeling well."

Amy was a single mom with a young son. "Did her babysitter crap out on her again?"

Sandra nodded and washed her hands quickly. "I'll give you a hand. What do you need?"

Roxy took the coward's way out. "There's a new guy just sat down at the counter. Can you get him for me while I deliver these?"

"Sure."

Daniel's gaze burned into her skin as she walked past with the meals. She didn't have to look his way to know how hot he looked tonight. To know he wore that new shirt just for her.

She'd never finish her reading tonight. A part of her wished Daniel had never come to her workplace to distract her again. Another part was more than pleased to know he'd come looking for her.

"What can I get'cha, hon?"

Daniel had been watching Roxy cross the room with two plates loaded with delicious-looking food. He'd been admiring her retreating figure. Her hips swayed seductively and he couldn't help but remember how they'd been pressed up against him on the dance floor not too long ago. He wanted to feel that again.

He knew he shouldn't have, but he'd applied a small

amount of the attraction elixir before he'd left the lab. That way he could call this another research session, not simply a desperate attempt to see Roxy again.

He turned around to see a large woman with bleached blonde hair and enormous hips standing in front of him, order pad and pen in hand.

"I...uh...I thought this was Roxy's section."

A smile spread across her heavily made-up face. "You know my Roxy?"

"Your Roxy?"

"I'm her mother, Sandy Erickson. I own this place."

"Oh, I didn't realize." But if he looked hard, he could see the resemblance in the green eyes and pretty smile. "I'm Daniel Jennings. I met Roxy at school."

Sandy shook her head. "Waste of time for that girl."

Daniel frowned. "Excuse me?"

"She's got a good job and a roof over her head. Now she's heaping all this extra work on her shoulders. To be a disc jockey?" Sandy rolled her eyes. "Why can't she realize she's got it good? Never could be satisfied with what she had, even as a kid."

"Um, well..."

"I know. She's a grown woman and I should keep my mouth shut. But if you're her friend, maybe you can try to get her to accept the fact that there is no shame in being a good waitress. The world needs waitresses, don't they? People want good restaurants to come to. Why can't she be happy with that?"

"Hey, Sandy, when you're done yapping, maybe you could bring me some more coffee?"

Daniel looked over at the old gentleman seated a couple of

bright red stools away from him. The small smile he was trying to hide let Daniel know he heard what Roxy's mother was saying. Daniel appreciated the distraction.

"Keep your shirt on, Charlie. I'll be there in a second."

"I'd take my shirt off for you any time, darlin'," Charlie said with a touch of affection in his voice.

Sandy's face turned red. "Get out of here. I got a business to run. Anyway, you've already had enough coffee to float a boat."

He winked at Daniel. "But if I went home, I wouldn't have this magnificent woman to look at."

"Get out of here," Sandy said again.

"Charlie, you still hitting on my mother?" Roxy said, coming around behind the counter. Daniel caught her eye and she smiled at him and made his day.

"She hasn't said yes, yet," Charlie said, yearning written all over his face. "I gotta keep trying."

Poor guy. Maybe he could slip a little of his formula Charlie's way.

The researcher in him reacted with horror. What was he thinking? He couldn't do anything like that. The testing wasn't anywhere near complete. He had no idea of the possible side effects. He couldn't be handing it out like candy to every Tom, Dick, or Charlie.

But Daniel understood the fondness and frustration Charlie was feeling. He glanced at Roxy and knew his face must hold that same look. He wished he had the courage to see her without the aid of his formula. What would they feel for each other then? Sooner or later, he was going to have to find out.

But not today.

"So, Doc, what did you decide?"

"Doc?" Roxy's mother said, her eyes growing wide. "This man is a doctor?"

"Easy, Mom. Dr. Jennings is a chemistry professor. He's a scientist."

Sandy shrugged. "Well, the world needs scientists too, I suppose."

Roxy rolled her eyes. "My mother is very practical."

Sandy shook her finger at Roxy. "I raised you and a business single-handedly. Practical is all I had time for."

"I know, Mom." Roxy put her arm around her mother and hugged her. "I'll take Dr. Jennings' order. You can go help Ralph. If Amy doesn't get back here soon, though, I'll need help delivering orders."

Mrs. Erickson looked from Daniel to Roxy and back again. Then she nodded and tucked her order pad and pen into the pocket of her apron. "Okay, sweetie. Nice to meet you, Dr. Jennings."

Roxy watched her mother disappear into the kitchen. Then she turned back to Daniel and shrugged. "Sorry about that. My mother is pretty outspoken."

"Like her daughter."

"Well, I had a good teacher." She pulled her order pad out. "Did you really want some dinner?"

"Of course, I do. What do you recommend?"

"Special tonight is Salisbury steak, mashed potatoes and green beans."

"Talked me into it."

"Gravy on your potatoes?"

"Please."

"Something to drink?"

"Coffee."

"Why did you come here tonight?"

She looked up from the order pad and stared at him with those lovely green eyes. He almost told her it was for the food, but he didn't want to lie to her anymore than he already had. "I wanted to see you again."

She sighed. "Daniel..."

He held up his hands in a sign of surrender. She didn't want to see him in the same way he wanted to see her. Somehow she was able to resist the attraction, while he couldn't stop himself from seeing her again. More data for his notebook. He wished it didn't bother him as much as it did. "I know. I know. I don't have a chance with you. I'm not asking you out. I just wanted to see you again."

"I like you, Daniel. I really do." She placed her hand on his and he curled his fingers around hers. "I wish things could be different, but I just don't have time to date right now."

"Gina said you've sworn off dating until you get your degree."

"That's right."

"Not very practical is it?"

"Roxy!"

Her name was shouted out from a speaker somewhere above them. She started to pull away, but Daniel didn't release his grip. "Are you sure we can't work something out?"

"I have to get that," she said, but the sorrow in her eyes answered his question. "I'll turn in your order."

Daniel watched her walk away, then stared at the worn kitchen door as it swung shut behind her.

"So what do you think of our foxy Roxy?"

Daniel turned to see a man about his age sit on the stool

beside him. “Excuse me?”

“That Roxy. She’s something, isn’t she?” He raised his bushy eyebrows. “Yeah, she really serves you up good, if you know what I mean.”

Daniel froze. Until he met Roxy, he wouldn’t have said he had a violent bone in his body, but first he’d had the urge to deck her ex-husband, and now he could easily imagine wiping that goofy grin off this guy’s face.

“Shut up, Kurt,” Charlie called out from Daniel’s other side. “You’d like to think she’d serve you anything but dinner, but it’s not going to happen.”

“Yeah?” Kurt raised his chin in a defiant move. Perfect for an upper cut. “How do you know it never will?”

“’Cause Roxy’s got too much taste, that’s why.”

Laughter rose all around them. Evidently most of the people here knew each other.

“Yeah, well, who does she think she is,” Kurt asked in a whiny voice. “Thinking she’s going to get a college degree after all this time? She spent all of high school with Todd Morgan on the brain. What makes her think she can get through college now?”

“Well, boy,” Charlie replied. “I don’t think there’s anything wrong with letting the girl try. I imagine sooner or later she’ll quit and come back here for good, but she’s gotta figure that out on her own.”

Anger flared up so quickly in Daniel, it surprised him. “You folks don’t have too much faith in her, do you?”

“Now don’t get me wrong, I love that little girl like she was my own. I watched her grow up here. Restaurant work is all she knows, and she’s damn good at it. But bookwork was never easy for her. I hate to see her get her dreams all dashed, but I’m afraid that's what's going to happen."

Daniel watched Roxy carry a tray of plates down to the other end of the restaurant, expertly dodging patrons getting out of their seats, beaming her sweet smile and talking to customers as she went. He hadn't known her for long, but he knew she was determined. And now he understood why she didn't want anything distracting her from her studies. "Or she just might surprise you all."

Chapter Six

As closing time neared, Charlie and Daniel were the only ones still in the diner. Roxy glanced up from wiping tables to see them chatting amiably. Amy had finally come back and that had taken the pressure off, but knowing Daniel was sitting at the counter, watching her with those warm eyes and smiling that lopsided smile, made her forget all about the reading she needed to get done tonight.

He sure was a powerful distraction.

Roxy walked back behind the counter and tossed the washcloth in the sink. Then she turned and slapped her hands down on the counter in front of Daniel. "Don't you have to get home and blow up something in your laboratory?"

A slow grin spread across his face. He shook his head. "I do my lab work at the school."

"No test tubes to wash?"

He laughed. What a warm, sexy sound. She wanted to laugh with him, but she frowned instead.

"None."

"Well, you must have to write up a pop quiz to torture your students with."

Daniel's eyes shone with amusement. "Are you trying to get rid of me?"

"Well, you've been monopolizing that stool all night. What if someone else wanted a seat?"

Daniel lifted an eyebrow and looked around him. The place was empty.

Roxy grinned. She couldn't help it. She'd enjoyed work more tonight than she had in years, and it was all because Daniel was there. "Never mind. Sit there as long as you want." She glanced at her watch. "Or at least for another fifteen minutes."

Amy came out of the kitchen. "Thanks for covering for me tonight. Scott's been running a fever off and on and I was worried."

"I know. It's okay." Roxy knew how hard it was to be a single mother, with no one to share the workload and responsibilities. That had been the story of her mother's life. Amy's life would be a whole lot easier if she had a good man.

She froze and stared at Amy.

Daniel was looking for a good woman. Wasn't that what Friday night was all about? Roxy pasted a smile on her face. "Hey, Doc. Did you get a chance to meet Amy Barnes? She's a good friend of mine."

Daniel smiled at Amy and Roxy swallowed to wash the bitter taste from her mouth.

"Hello, Amy," he said softly.

"Amy, this is Dr. Daniel Jennings. He's a chemistry professor at CSU."

Amy blushed an attractive shade of pink. "Nice to meet you, Dr. Jennings."

"Please, call me Daniel." His voice sounded smoother and sexier than it had ever sounded when he was talking to Roxy. She was certain of it. He held out his hand to shake Amy's and continued to hold it even after all the shaking was done.

"Well, Daniel," Amy gushed, "would you believe chemistry was my favorite subject in high school?"

Roxy didn't believe it. She also didn't believe Amy was actually batting her eyes at Daniel. Why on earth did she think she should match these two up? If they hit it off, she'd be tortured by Daniel hanging around the diner for Amy.

"How long have you worked with Roxy?" Daniel asked.

"Oh, gosh, ten years?"

"Well, you certainly don't look old enough to have worked anywhere for that long."

Amy giggled and Roxy turned away before she puked. She reminded herself that this was what she wanted. She had no business feeling upset or nasty or, God forbid, jealous. The whole point of the past few days was to find a woman for Daniel. She never imagined he and Amy would hit it off this quickly, that was all. She may have introduced them, but she didn't have to stay and listen to all this...this shit.

She went back into the kitchen and helped Ralph and Paulie clean up. When she finally peeked out front, her mom was sitting at the counter with Charlie, schedule sheets spread out in front of her. And Daniel was sitting by himself.

"Where's Amy?" Roxy asked.

"I let her go," her mom replied. "She wanted to get home to Scott."

Daniel looked at her and a little nervous tickle suddenly fluttered in her stomach. She couldn't tell what he was thinking. Was he mad at her for trying to set him up with Amy? Or was his body buzzing with desire as much as hers was?

She propped her hands on her hips and tried to look irritated. "You still here?"

"Thought you might need a ride home." he said, standing.

She usually caught a bus or cab to work and bummed a ride home with her mother. "Thanks, but I get a ride with my mom."

Daniel shrugged casually. "I don't mind. It's on my way."

She shouldn't get into that sexy sports car with him. It would be like asking for temptation. But her mother was still working on next week's schedule and Roxy knew she might get home quicker if she took Daniel up on his offer.

"You sure you don't mind?" She looked into his heated gaze and knew she wasn't even fooling herself.

A slow smile spread across his face. "Of course not."

A new flood of awareness washed over her. She nodded. Her hands actually shook as she untied her apron and threw it in the hamper. "Mom, I'll get a ride home with Daniel."

Sandy looked up from the papers in front of her. "Are you sure?"

"Yeah. It's okay. Daniel gave me a ride home from school the other night."

Sandy stared at them for a moment, probably wondering what was going on between them. Then she nodded and turned her attention back to the schedule.

Daniel took Roxy's hand in his warm, solid one and led her out the door. The autumn wind whipped around them, cool against her heated skin. The inky darkness was dispersed by a single spotlight at the far end of the parking lot.

When they rounded the front of the building and turned back into the parking lot, Daniel moaned. "Roxy."

He whirled her around and pushed her back up against the side of the building. Her hands flew up in surprise and he pinned them against the wall with his own hands.

Her heart pounded and her breath came in quick pants. Wow. This wasn't the confused man with the puppy dog eyes she'd met a few days ago. There was a take-charge side of him she'd never seen before. Where had he come from, this Daniel who took her breath away?

His face was shadowed and when he stepped closer, pressing the hard length of him against her body, she couldn't see at all. She could only feel.

Feel his breath on her face, warm and soft on her skin. His hands on hers, strong and secure, their fingers laced together. His hard cock pressed into her stomach, leaving no doubt of his attraction to her.

Her body arched against his, acknowledging his desire. Showing him her own. She'd been fooling herself all along. It didn't matter if the time was right or not. She wanted this man with every inch of her body, with every breath she drew, with every thought in her jumbled mind.

"I've been thinking about doing this all night long," he whispered. Then he lightly brushed his lips over hers, just enough to tickle, just enough to tease. "It was driving me nuts to watch you and not touch you."

"Daniel." She couldn't say anything more than his name. Couldn't think of anything more than that she needed to taste him. Touch him. Feel his hands on her body. His mouth on her skin.

He released her hands and she combed her fingers into his hair, bringing his face to hers. He crushed his lips to hers, hard and hot. She opened her mouth under him, opened herself up to him, and he plunged his tongue between her lips. She tasted coffee and something else that must have been Daniel. Had she ever tasted anything that good? She sucked on his tongue, drinking in his unique taste. He moaned and pressed more tightly against her.

He skimmed his hands along her ribs and over her hips. "I've been fantasizing about your curves since the moment I met you."

Yeah, she had curves, all right. Overly abundant curves. But Daniel didn't make it sound like a bad thing. She couldn't help but smile. "Oh, really?"

"Mmm." He brought his caresses back up to her waist. "Very sexy curves." He caught her mouth again with his.

Her pulse skipped. Her breath caught. Desire pooled deep inside her.

Dear God, he made her feel sexy.

Daniel tried to find a way to slip his hands beneath her blouse, then he must have realized that she was wearing a dress tonight. No cloth to pull out of the waistband. He cursed in frustration, the words lost in her mouth.

Laughter bubbled up from that pool of need gathering within her. She guided his hands to the buttons that ran up the front of her dress. She tried to help him undo them, but their fingers tangled together. She laughed again when one of the buttons popped.

It seemed to take forever until his hands were finally on her breasts, cupping them with his palms. He rubbed the balls of his thumbs over her lace-covered nipples and waves of panty-dampening desire swept through her, strong and steady, even though her bra was still in the way.

Arousal tugged from her nipples straight to her core. It had been so long since she'd been this turned on. Had she ever been this turned on? Moisture gathered between her legs. He slid one of his thighs between her legs and she rubbed herself against him.

God. That was so good. She hadn't realized how much she needed this. She moaned and slid her hands up his chest and around his neck. He bent his head down and nuzzled his face between her breasts.

She heard the front door of the restaurant slam. Daniel must have heard it too, because he froze at the same instant she did, hands on her breasts, thigh between her legs. That would be Charlie leaving. She tried not to let a nervous giggle escape her lips.

Then she heard her mother's voice floating toward them on the evening breeze. Charlie must have been walking her to her car.

Roxy yanked Daniel tighter against her, hoping they would both be hidden in the shadows of the building. The humor in the situation was not lost to her that the two of them, way old enough to know better, were necking in the parking lot like a couple of teenagers. She'd never necked in public in her life, not even when she was dating Todd in high school, although her mother had imagined all sorts of things, most of the rest of them true. That her mother might catch her now, at her age, was even more ironic. Laughter threatened to burst out of her. She bent her head down to smother her giggles in Daniel's hair.

His face was still buried in her chest. She felt him start to shake and she realized he was laughing too.

"Shhh," she whispered in his ear. But the giggles threatened to escape and she pressed her mouth against his neck. Man, he smelled good. She slipped her tongue out between her lips and licked his skin.

He tasted good too.

She heard Charlie and her mother talking. She couldn't make out the words, but it sounded like Charlie was trying to convince her again to go out with him. It was so ridiculous, really. He'd been hanging around the restaurant and asking her mother out for as long as Roxy could remember.

But her mother was the practical one. She didn't believe in love any more than Roxy did. They'd both had husbands leave them. They'd both learned the hard way never to let their happiness depend on a man.

But Roxy started to wonder if she couldn't simply take a man up on what he was offering. She'd gone through lots of years of mediocre sex, letting Todd get away with the excuse of being tired because of his heavy class load. She realized she'd never been as aroused during sex with Todd as she was after one heavy kiss with Daniel.

If it wasn't for her own crazy class load, Roxy would jump at the chance to take Daniel up on his offer. But the simple fact was that if she ever wanted to get out of the restaurant, she had to concentrate on her studies.

Damn, she'd really love to go farther than they could at the edge of the parking lot. But she had to keep her priorities straight.

Finally, she heard two car doors slam. Two engines start up. Two cars drive away. Luckily, the parking lot exit was at the opposite end from where they were standing, or the headlights would have lit up the two of them in their clinch like two startled deer.

Daniel stepped away from her, still laughing lightly. Roxy let herself laugh out loud and slowly slid her back down the wall until she was sitting in the small strip of grass that ringed the building. Daniel sat beside her.

"I feel like a teenager almost getting caught making out," Roxy said.

"Well, you almost did. Get caught, I mean." He laughed. "We both did."

She took a deep breath and let it out slowly. "Yeah."

They didn't talk for a moment and their breathing slowly returned to normal. Of course, sitting next to the man she had the hots for, with the front of her dress hanging open, her skin tingling with need, there was no way she would be breathing exactly normally.

"We could go someplace where we wouldn't get caught," Daniel said, the smooth, seductive tone of his voice sliding over her like hot fudge.

Oh, but she was tempted.

He ran his hand slowly down her arm until he reached her hand. He entwined her fingers with his and placed their arms gently across his knee. "We can go to my place. I don't have a roommate."

She dropped her head back, almost hitting it on the brick wall behind her. "Daniel..."

Dry leaves skittered across the blacktop. He squeezed her hand and let it go. She almost cried out with the loss, but she knew she couldn't have it both ways.

"Were you trying to set me up with Amy back there?" Daniel asked suddenly. She thought she heard a touch of amusement in his voice. Or was it annoyance?

"She needs a good man," she told him. "You're a good man. You need a good woman, and she is."

"I'm sure she is, but somehow I can't picture Amy sitting in the dark with me like this."

"I can't picture *you* sitting in the dark with me like this."

"I have to admit this is a first for me."

"Doc, listen..."

"No." He smoothed his fingers down her cheek and she couldn't pretend that it didn't feel wonderful. He pressed his fingers against her lips. "Every time you call me Doc, you're trying to distance yourself from me. Don't do that. Tell me the truth. Tell me what you feel. I need to know."

She sighed. "You know I'm attracted to you. I don't seem to have control over it."

He continued to stroke her face and didn't say a word.

"You know I like kissing you," she went on. "Wow, do I like kissing you. I wish we could keep going, but we can't, Daniel. I have to concentrate on my education right now. If I don't pass these classes, I can kiss my chances of ever getting out of this place good-bye. And my career in radio will be nothing but a dream." She sighed. "School is hard for me. I wish it wasn't, but it is. It's never come easy. I need to work hard just to get okay grades. If I let myself get distracted, I might as well quit right now."

"You're not going to quit," Daniel said, his voice more forceful than she ever heard it before. "I'll help you with your schoolwork."

"Oh, Daniel, I don't want you to do that."

"But I can help you. I want to help you. If it makes you feel better, you can consider it paying you back for the dancing lessons."

But she wanted to do it by herself. She had to know she could make it on her own, without a man's help. "I'll be okay as long as I don't get distracted."

"Okay." He leaned over her and started buttoning up her dress.

She brought up her hands to help, and their fingers got tangled together again. Roxy pulled him toward her and kissed him lightly. "Thanks."

Just then, the back door of the restaurant slammed. Of

course, Ralph and Paulie. Roxy pulled her knees up to her chest so that her bright white sneakers wouldn't be hanging out on the blacktop. Daniel drew his legs up also and put his arm around her. He leaned his face into her neck.

"Here we go again," he whispered.

She couldn't stop the giggles this time. They bubbled up and out of her. She turned her face into Daniel's shoulder to stifle the sound. He gathered her to him and his soft laughter blew warm against her ear.

She heard Ralph and Paulie talking, but she couldn't make out their words any more than she could her mom's and Charlie's. Her laughter stopped in her throat as she became aware of Daniel, wrapped around her like a blanket. His heat enveloped her. His scent surrounded her.

What was she going to do about him? She couldn't even pretend that she thought of him as Doc right now. He was Daniel, the man she was attracted to. She couldn't fight it. She didn't even want to.

But she had to. She had to walk away from him. Stay away from him. She had to leave him free to find a woman who wasn't committed to four years of school. A woman who didn't struggle every day to finish the schoolwork, the restaurant work, the housework. He needed a woman who would have room in her life for him. Not someone too exhausted most of the time to even stay awake.

Tears began to well in her eyes. Oh, great, just what she needed, for Daniel to see her crying. She rubbed her face against his neck, the soft collar of his shirt wiping away any lingering moisture. She heard two cars drive off and reluctantly pulled away from Daniel's embrace.

She forced a smile. "Whew, that was close. Thank goodness they didn't see us here."

Daniel rose and helped her to her feet. "Well, just because they didn't see us, doesn't mean they didn't know we were here somewhere."

"What do you mean?"

He pointed to his Porsche. It was the only car in the otherwise deserted parking lot.

Roxy looked away from the telltale car to Daniel's bright eyes. She shrugged. "Oh, well. Not much we can do about it now. But I bet I hear about it tomorrow."

"You're a grown woman," Daniel said. He slid his hand up her arm, sending light shivers in its wake. "You can make out with anyone you want."

"I know. But these guys are like big brothers to me. Or protective uncles. They look out for me."

"Then we better get you home," he said with a chuckle, "before they come back with a shotgun."

Roxy let out a short bark of laughter.

Daniel turned to her. "What? Don't tell me they would actually do that sort of thing?"

"Well, I probably shouldn't admit this to you, but since we've survived almost getting caught together, I guess I should tell you about the time I did get caught."

The wind kicked up again and she shivered. Daniel wrapped his arm around her shoulder and she leaned against him. "It was with Todd, of course. High school graduation night. My bedroom. We were trying to be so quiet, but Mom still heard us. She slammed the door open so hard I thought the house was falling down. There we were, caught in the act, with Mom shouting at Todd to get his bony ass out of her house before she killed him."

"I imagine your mother would be quite intimidating in that

situation," Daniel said wryly.

"You can say that again." She couldn't believe she was actually blushing from the memory. Her mom had been so pissed. And so disappointed. "I don't know exactly what Charlie, Ralph, and Paulie said to Todd, or if a shotgun was involved, but he proposed to me a couple days later and we were married before he started college."

"Did you love him?"

She sighed. "Passionately. As truly as an eighteen-year-old can love before real life fucks things up."

"Forgive me for asking, but why did you stay with him so long then?"

"Because I made a commitment, damn it! Because I took a vow."

Daniel brushed his lips across her ear and she accepted the comfort he offered. "He didn't deserve your loyalty."

"No, he didn't."

She'd been determined to make her marriage work, even if it had been single-handedly. Todd's reasons for staying were pretty simple. Roxy took care of the bills, the housework, everything that had to be done so Todd could get his education. So he could get good grades and get his degree. Pass his bar. Then he'd promised he'd start paying the bills so she could go back to school.

Roxy went into it with her eyes open. They'd talked it over and she'd agreed it was the smart thing to do. But she hadn't known Todd wasn't planning to spend his future with her. He'd make a good politician, someday. He had been an expert at empty promises. He said whatever he thought Roxy wanted to hear. Then he went and did whatever he wanted anyway. With whomever he wanted to do it with.

"Ready to go?"

Daniel's voice shook her out of the unpleasant memories. The ones that made her feel like a fool. Enough of that.

"Yeah. It's getting cold out here."

Daniel turned her around into the circle of his arms. "My apartment is nice and warm."

She moaned and leaned into him. "Don't tempt me."

He stroked her back slowly with his warm hands. Shivers of awareness ran along her skin and she wanted to feel more.

"I'm tempting, am I?" he asked.

"You know you are." She stepped out of the warmth of his arms before she did what she longed to do. "You'd better take me home."

"Hey, Dr. Jennings. Can I talk to you for a minute?"

Daniel set aside the notes he was making on the potion. He hadn't gotten very far this afternoon. He kept thinking about Roxy, kept tasting her on his lips, feeling her hands on his body and her body under his hands.

One of his third-year students, Kent McLaughlin, strode into the room. Tall and thin, gawky even, he reminded Daniel a lot of himself at that age.

"Hey, Kent. What can I do for you?"

Kent shook his hand with a firm grip. "I wanted to thank you for the letter of recommendation you wrote. I always wanted to study overseas. I can't believe I was accepted."

"I don't find it at all hard to believe," Daniel told him. "You're an excellent student and I have every confidence you will be a fine chemist. I'm glad you have this opportunity."

A blush spread across Kent's face, turning it nearly as red as his hair. "Yeah, well, thanks to your help and encouragement."

"Thanks to all the hard work you've done," Daniel told him. "You realize I expect regular e-mails next semester while you're away."

Kent grinned. His freckled face lit up. "You got it, Dr. Jennings."

Daniel's cell phone rang. He patted his pockets. Where was the damn thing? He could hear it playing the "William Tell Overture", but he had no idea where he'd put it.

Kent bent down and flipped opened Daniel's briefcase sitting beside his desk. He grabbed the phone and handed it to Daniel. "Here you go. See you later."

Daniel waved and then answered the phone before checking the caller ID. He immediately wished it was still buried in his briefcase. He wasn't in the mood for an argument with his father.

"Hi, Dad."

"I've been leaving you messages for a week. Don't you ever check them?"

"When I have the time." Had he even checked his messages since he met Roxy?

Never one for small talk, his father started right in. "I don't know how long that opening here will be available. You'll have to get your application in right away. Now I've talked to the powers that be and you're practically guaranteed the position. But, son, you have to apply."

Daniel stifled a sigh and sank into his chair. His parents had been after him for years to work with them. "I appreciate you thinking of me for the position, but I'm just not interested in pharmaceutical research."

"How can you say that?" Daniel could picture his father pacing in his den, an incredulous look on his face. "You'd be working with the best minds in the country. You'll have state-of-the-art equipment at your disposal."

"The university's equipment is great."

"State-funded equipment? Don't be ridiculous. You have no idea what great equipment is."

"Dad..."

"You'll be making a real difference in people's lives, Daniel. We're this close...this close to finding a cancer vaccine. It's an exciting time. You can be part of that. Your life will be worth something."

Even though they'd had this same conversation countless times, the words still burned like acid in his stomach. "And my life now is worth nothing?" Daniel asked.

"Of course not, but fitness formulas?" The condescension was clear in his father's voice. "You call that a benefit to mankind?"

"Yes, I think making people feel better about themselves benefits mankind. And I'm a college professor. A teacher. I can think of no greater benefit than teaching the next generation of scientists."

"But you could be saving lives."

Daniel knew his father wouldn't understand. Even if he told him that Kent, heading overseas next semester, tried to commit suicide his freshman year because he didn't fit in. Didn't have any friends. Didn't feel he had a reason to go on living. Daniel knew he wasn't solely responsible for Kent's turnaround, but he was glad he'd recognized the young man's despair in time.

He'd helped Kent find his way back through his love of chemistry, asking for Kent's help on some lab experiments and encouraging him to do some of his own science projects. And look at him now.

Daniel hoped he'd touched other lives as well over the years, but he'd probably never know. How many students might take something they learned from him and make a difference in the world? The possibility—and the responsibility—was never far from Daniel's mind.

"I have to go now, Dad. Tell Mom I said hi." Daniel disconnected before his father had a chance to say anything else. He knew that only *he* had the power to make himself feel unworthy. But somehow his father had always managed to wield that power as well.

Was he really wasting his time? Wasting his life? Could he be doing something more productive? More important?

He had his own experiments, in addition to his teaching. His protein supplement had a large market. But no one could compare that to curing cancer.

And now he was working on a frivolous pheromone formula. One that he started to develop after his breakup with Cynthia. He knew there had to be an easier way to find the right person. A way to boost the natural attraction between a man and a woman and find the passion that had been missing from his life.

He didn't know any other way than through scientific research.

He thought at first he'd pinpointed the correct formula, but although Roxy was attracted to him, she still resisted his advances. What did that mean? Was this another variable he had to add to the equation? Did it mean that Roxy wasn't the right person for him? He didn't want to believe that.

So was it possible that his formula didn't work? Or even if it did work, did it not attract the right person? Was he wasting his time?

Damn his father for making him question his life and his choices, with every conversation, every backhanded compliment he made.

Daniel snatched up his cell phone and hurled it across the room. It hit the wall beside the door and smashed into hundreds of pieces.

Gina barely missed being hurt by flying debris. She stopped in the doorway and lifted an eyebrow. "Whoa, Dr. Jennings. Bad day?"

Daniel sighed and shook his head. That was a stupid reaction. He got a broom and dust pan from the closet. "Something like that," he mumbled.

She took the dust pan from him and scooped up the pieces he swept into it. Daniel took the broken pieces of his cell phone and dumped them in the trash. Well, that was a complete waste of time. He didn't feel any better and now he was going to have to get a new cell phone.

He reached for his jacket. He had to get out of here for a while.

"Dr. Jennings, can I talk to you for a minute?" Gina asked. "About the love potion."

Not the love potion. Anything but the love potion. "I'm sorry, Gina. I can't right now. But we'll talk soon, all right? I promise."

He put his hand into his jacket pocket as he walked out the door. The vial was still there.

An F?

Roxy sat in the hard plastic chair and stared at the algebra test the professor had just handed back to her. Red X's were scratched on every sheet. Her hand shook and she dropped the papers onto the desk. The big red letter at the top of the page blurred in front of her.

How the hell did she get an F?

Yeah, she knew she wasn't going to get an A. Or even a B. But an F? That was so unfair. She'd tried really hard. She'd studied and studied for this test. Her brain hurt for hours afterward.

The professor was droning on about the next assignment, but she couldn't understand a word he said. She couldn't make sense of anything. One glance around the room let her know that she was the only one staring at her test grade with disbelief.

Was she fooling herself? Maybe she should listen to her mother and drop her dream of a college education. Maybe it just wasn't for her. All these young kids could pass this test with flying colors. Why couldn't she? When it came to algebra she just didn't have a clue. Math had never been easy for her. But an F?

She straightened her shoulders and took a deep breath. She couldn't give up yet. Maybe if she studied harder. Longer.

She knew she'd be an awesome DJ. She was really getting into the courses for her major, like public speaking and fundamentals of communication. Her grades in those courses were better than she'd hoped. But math was one of the core requirements. If she couldn't pass algebra, she'd never get her degree. It was as simple as that.

The class was filing out. She made a quick note of the page numbers written on the board and bolted from the room. It was nearly dark already. Her last class of the day. She was meeting Gina in the cafeteria. They'd planned to grab a bite to eat before heading home but Roxy knew she wouldn't be able to eat anything. Her stomach was tied in knots. Negative thoughts kept flying through her head, telling her to give it up now. It was no use. Why put herself through all the work and misery for nothing?

Gina was lounging at a little table in the corner, wolfing down a cheeseburger. Roxy grabbed a cola to ease her queasy stomach and slumped into the seat across from her.

"You look like hell," Gina said.

"I feel like hell."

Gina put down her cheeseburger and sat up straight. "What's wrong?"

Roxy wasn't ready to say the words out loud. She couldn't admit to Gina that she was failing algebra. Gina was one of the smartest women she knew. She'd act like she understood, but she wouldn't. She'd feel sorry for her, and that was the last thing Roxy wanted.

"I've got a lot on my mind. I...um, I need to talk to Dr. Jennings." She had to see him now, while her mind was still in a panic mode and she'd be less likely to weaken. "Can you wait for me here? I'm going to run over to his lab for a sec. I'll be right back."

Gina shook her head. "He's gone. I can't believe he's actually going home at a decent hour. What did you do to him?"

"I didn't do anything." But she had to do this now, before she got in any deeper. "I have to see him. Do you know where he lives?"

"Yeah. I'll give you the address." Gina chewed thoughtfully for a moment. "I don't get it. You ought to look a little happier to be seeing a handsome, smart nice guy like Dr. Jennings."

Roxy resisted the urge to roll her eyes. “I’m not seeing him, Gina. I just need to see him.”

Gina shrugged. “Yeah. Right. Whatever you say.”

Chapter Seven

Roxy stood in the lobby of the plush apartment building and her stomach sank to her knees. Gina's directions were right on the money, but shit, was she ever in the wrong place. If she ever needed proof that she and Daniel did not belong together, this was it.

Look at this place, with its plush draperies and marble floors. There was an honest-to-goodness security guard who sat behind a massive desk and wouldn't let her through without an okay from the Doc. She'd known he had to have money—he drove a Porsche for heaven's sake. But seeing where he lived drove home the fact that he was really rich, not just some guy who liked to splurge on a car.

Their differences had never slapped her in the face quite like they did right now.

He was a rich, intelligent scientist with doctor in front of his name. She was a waitress in a diner who lived in a second floor walk-up and struggled simply to pass her freshman classes. Who was failing one of her freshman classes.

She looked down at her scuffed loafers and was about ready to turn tail and get out of this joint when the security guard put down the telephone. "You can go right up to the fifth floor, Miss. Dr. Jennings is waiting for you."

She nodded and tried to ignore the sudden tickles in her

belly. What was that all about? She'd never been nervous seeing Daniel before. Was it because she now realized the huge differences standing between them? Or because of what she knew she had to say to him?

She took a deep breath. Enough stalling. Time to get this over with. "Thank you."

The elevator slid silently up from the lobby. When the doors opened, she was surprised to see Daniel standing right there waiting for her. Now she didn't have any time to think about what she was going to say. He was smiling like he was glad to see her. She had to stop that right away.

She didn't quite meet his eye, but looked over his shoulder. "Hey, Doc, nice digs."

He frowned. "We're back to Doc, I see."

She shrugged and walked past him, careful not to touch him. She couldn't touch him. She was afraid if she did, she'd never stop. She'd forget what she came here to say. And the reason why. She turned to the right and started to walk down the hallway. "I need to talk to you for a second."

"Sure." He put his hand on her shoulder and spun her around. "My place is down this way."

"Oh, okay." Why did he have to touch her? She'd spent all day trying to forget the way his warm hands felt when they skimmed over her skin. Trying to pay attention to lectures instead of replaying the previous night in her mind. Trying to come up with the right words to say to him now.

"I didn't expect to see you tonight," Daniel said. He pushed open a heavy wooden door and ushered her inside. "But I'm certainly glad you're here."

"Wow, this is a nice place." She walked ahead of him into a spacious living room. Black and tan leather furniture shared the space with glass-topped tables and chrome lamps. A bank of windows stretched across the back wall. The lights of Cowden twinkled before her and she thought she could even see the lake in the distance. "Awesome view."

Daniel stopped beside her, almost touching her, but not quite. "I'm not here enough to enjoy it all that much. Mostly just to eat take-out and sleep."

His words brought to mind the fact that Daniel's bed was here somewhere. Somewhere close. Was the bed big? Would the sheets smell like him?

She closed her eyes and breathed in his spicy scent. Why did this have to be so hard?

"Can I get you something to drink?" he asked. "Are you hungry? I've got leftover Chinese in the refrigerator."

He'd never know how hungry she was. She opened her eyes and feasted on him. Memorized his features. Took in all the little details she was already hooked on. After all, she might never see him again after tonight.

She hadn't known him all that long, for heaven's sake. It shouldn't be a big deal to break up what hadn't really even started yet.

She cleared her throat. "No, thanks. I just have something I need to say to you and then I'll be out of your hair."

"You're not in my hair." He gestured toward a long, black leather sofa. "Have a seat."

She shook her head and started pacing around the room. No way could she sit still and do this.

"Okay," he said. "What's on your mind?"

"I like you a lot, Daniel." Shit, that's probably not the way she should have started. He'd get the wrong idea right off the bat.

"I'm glad." He studied her, obviously wondering what she

was getting at. "I like you too. I like the way you kiss. I like the way you dance. I like the way you speak your mind."

She stopped pacing and waved her hand in front of his face. "Shhh. Let me finish. I can't see you any more. Not even as friends."

He put his hands on her shoulders, gently squeezing her tired muscles. Damn, he was touching her again. He made her want to lean into him. And made her want to touch him back.

She stepped away, putting needed space between them.

"I don't have that many friends," he said softly. "I'd hate to lose even one. Especially you."

She crossed the room and stared out over the city. The lights sparkled like colored jewels. Her apartment looked over a used car lot. "We don't belong together. We don't have anything in common."

He came up behind her. "I've heard that opposites attract."

She waved his words away again. "We're so far past opposite it's not funny. You have an elevator, for heaven's sake."

"You're not making any sense."

"I don't have to make sense to you. Just to me. And it's not just our differences."

But now that the time had come, she couldn't bring herself to tell him about the F. She didn't want him to think she was stupid. She wasn't stupid. She just couldn't grasp binomial coefficients and linear polynomials and all those other wacko terms. So all she could offer him was the same old, same old.

"I have plans, you know? I've been looking forward to going back to school for a long time now. You're too distracting. We've gone over all of this before, but this time I'm really serious. I have goals. I have a broadcast booth with my name on it and I can't focus on all that when my mind is full of you."

She steeled herself for the argument she thought would follow her declaration. But Daniel didn't seem to be upset with her. Instead, he smiled and gathered her into his arms before she could stop him.

"So your mind is full of me, is it?"

She pretended to pummel his shoulders with her fists, but somehow her arms wrapped around his neck. "Stop sounding so smug. I can't concentrate on anything else. I've got to take a step back here. I need to spend some time away from you. Focus on my class work."

"Let me help you with your studies, Roxy. I'll be happy to."

She shook her head. "It won't work. I'll see you." She brushed her fingers across his cheek. "I'll, um, I'll smell you. I'll touch you. And I'll forget all about algebra equations or public speaking essays, or..." She rubbed her lips lightly over his and forgot whatever else she was going to say.

"Roxy." Her name sounded like a sigh coming from his lips. His gaze swept over her, the warm intensity of it making her feel desirable. Attractive. Wanted. But instead of kissing her as she expected, he stepped away from her, taking away his warmth. "I understand what you're saying. And you're right. It's wrong of me to try to distract you. I know how important an education is to you."

She nodded. "It is, Daniel. It really is."

"I have an idea."

"What?"

"I know someone who could tutor you. One of my students. She's a smart kid, but very insecure. I think helping someone else would give her ego a boost. What do you say? I can talk to her in the morning."

"Oh, um, I'll think about it." Why did she feel disappointed? Daniel had listened to her, respected her feelings and thought of a solution to help her. What woman wouldn't love her man to do that?

He wasn't her man! She wanted to shake herself. She couldn't have it both ways. She couldn't be upset that she told Daniel she couldn't see him anymore and he actually honored her decision. What was wrong with her?

"I'm not happy with the part where we don't see each other anymore," Daniel went on as if he could read her mind. "But I promise not to seek you out. You'll have to come to me."

She couldn't say anything as he put his arm around her shoulder and led her toward the front door.

"I hope you can find room in your life for me and school." He stopped at the door and turned her to face him. "You see, I like the fact that you're thinking about me all the time. I think about you all the time too. I hope you'll keep thinking about me."

He pulled her to him and lowered his lips to hers, searing her with his hot mouth. Just as she began to soften and lean against him, he lifted his lips and stepped away from her. "You'll have to come to me."

He opened the front door to his apartment and gently shoved her out into the hallway.

"Think about me," he said. And closed the door in her face.

Metallica blasted through the speakers. Roxy let the bass line throb through her as she searched for the right words to give the finish of her essay a punch. Gina had gone out on another first date. Mr. and Mrs. Campbell were out for their weekly bingo fix. She'd cranked up the music as loud as she could, but she still couldn't get Daniel out of her mind.

She threw down a tooth-marked pencil. It wasn't fair. She'd done everything she could think of to keep her mind on her schoolwork. She still kept thinking about Daniel like she was some teeny-bopper with her first crush. She barely made it through high school because she was hung up on Todd Morgan. She wasn't going to make the same mistake twice.

She shook her head, wiping Daniel's warm hazel eyes out of her head. She scribbled the last paragraph of her essay and closed the notebook. Now she just had to get to the computer lab in the morning to type it up before class.

With a groan, she picked up the dreaded algebra book and opened to the assignment. The numbers and symbols stared back at her. Why did she care about algebra? She could add up a meal order and figure the tax. She could balance her checkbook and order supplies for the restaurant. What else did she need math for? What good was algebra?

Roxy dropped the book and stared at it in horror. Oh, God, she sounded like her mother. There had to be a reason she needed algebra.

She stood and punched a fist in the air. Because it was there, that's why. Like Mount Everest. She wanted to expand her knowledge. She wanted a degree and a career she could look forward to. She sank back onto the sofa.

Too bad she hated math.

She stared at the page again. She thought this had all made sense when the professor explained it in class. But at the moment, she didn't have a clue. If she wasn't careful, she was going to fail another test. Maybe she'd take Daniel up on that tutoring help after all.

And there she was, thinking about Daniel again.

She was still staring at the page of problems when Gina came flying through the door. She grabbed the remote and turned the volume on the radio down to nearly inaudible.

"You'll be deaf by the time you're thirty," Gina told her.

Roxy tipped her head to the side. "What?"

"I said—oh, you think you're so cute!" Gina threw the remote down on the table. The tension in her voice made her sound as if she was ready to explode.

Roxy had been about to break into a big smile, instead she studied Gina. Her roommate's face was red and tear-stained. Roxy jumped to her feet. "You look awful. What happened? Are you okay?"

"Oh, Randy Ames is a jerk. An asshole. A bastard. I should have known better than to go out with a guy with his reputation."

Anger mixed with fear flared in Roxy's stomach. "He didn't hurt you, did he?"

"Just my feelings." Gina peeled off her bright pink fleece jacket and hung it over the back of the chair. "He said some awful things cuz I wouldn't go down on him in the movie theater."

Roxy clenched her hands into fists. "Let's go beat him up."

Gina shook her head, but a little grin popped out. "No. That's okay. I just have to consider the source, right?"

Roxy threw her arms around Gina and gave her a big hug. "What an asshole. Whatever made you go out with him to begin with?"

Gina shrugged and walked into the kitchen. "He just came up to me and asked me out with a great big smile, flashing those blue eyes and little dimple. I thought I'd give it a try. My mistake." She grabbed a package of microwave popcorn out of the cupboard. "Hey, let's nuke some popcorn and bitch about guys."

Roxy would have liked to complain to Gina about the way Daniel used that last kiss against her. He had to know she'd keep reliving the taste of him on her lips. She still felt the sweet pressure of his lips against hers, still felt his warm hands on her body. And she yearned for more. After three days she still thought about it constantly.

But she couldn't tell Gina that.

So Roxy glared at the books on the table in front of her. "As long as I can bitch about algebra too."

"Deal."

They'd just settled at the coffee table with a huge bowl of extra-butter popcorn when there was a knock at the door. Roxy licked the greasy butter off her fingers as she got up and went to the door.

"Mom?" Roxy could count on one hand the number of times her mother had hiked up the long, steep stairs to this apartment. Her mother's breathing was coming in gasps. Roxy opened the door wide. "Come on in."

Her mother clasped one hand to her chest, a vinyl bag hanging from her fist. She held onto the door jamb with her other hand as she slowly entered the apartment.

"Hey, Mrs. Erickson," Gina called from across the room.

Her mother nodded at Gina and continued to gasp for breath.

"Mom? Are you all right?" With her extra weight, her mother usually breathed a little heavily, but Roxy had never seen her like this. A little twinge of fear snaked through her. She took her mother's arm and led her over to the sofa. "Here, sit down."

Sandra dropped onto the sofa. The worn springs groaned a little in protest. She swallowed, then said, “Why don’t you find a first-floor apartment?”

“Can’t afford it,” Roxy replied wryly. “You want some water?”

Sandra nodded. The large bag she’d carried in with her was still clasped to her chest. Roxy grabbed a glass of water and watched anxiously as her mother sipped on it.

“Are you okay?” Roxy asked again, hovering.

“I hate stairs,” her mother said. She groaned as she leaned forward to set the glass down on the table. Then she leaned back against the sofa cushions. Her breathing seemed to be back down to normal. “I’m okay now. Thank you for the water.” She smiled up at Roxy. “So. You’re seeing a doctor.”

Leave it to her mother. “Mom. I told you, he’s a college professor.”

“So. You’re seeing a college professor. That’s good, Roxy. I’m happy for you.”

“I’m not seeing him.”

“Yeah, she’s not seeing him and she’s blasting the music again,” Gina said.

Roxy turned and glared at Gina.

Her mother shook her head. “You know it’s not a bad thing, to be dating a doctor. He seems like a very nice man. You need a nice man, Roxy, there’s nothing wrong with that.”

“I didn’t say there was anything wrong with Daniel,” Roxy said. “I like him.”

“And he likes you too. I could tell.”

“Mom, I’m not dating Daniel. I’m not dating any one. I’ve told you a million times. I don’t have time. Not until I have my degree.”

"I know. I know," Sandra said. She patted the bag in her arms. "I came by to give you something. I was going to wait 'til Christmas. But I think you need it now." She held out the bag to Roxy. "Here."

Roxy frowned and took it from her. Whatever was in the bag was square and about the size of a serving tray. She opened the bag and slid out what looked like the back of a picture. Roxy flipped it over and saw it was a framed needlework. Colorful embroidered flowers surrounded the words "Bloom Where You Are Planted".

Roxy dropped the picture as if it had burned her. It landed with a thud on the coffee table, knocking over the bowl of popcorn. She stared at the kernels spilling over her feet.

How could she? How could her mother expect her to accept something with a sentiment like that? It was the complete opposite of everything Roxy was striving for. She didn't want to be stuck where she was. She certainly didn't want to be happy to be stuck here.

Gina jumped up and grabbed the picture out from under the avalanche of popcorn. She glanced at Roxy and then smiled at Sandra, obviously trying to cover for Roxy's rudeness. "Wow, Mrs. Erickson, did you make this?"

"Keeps my hands busy," her mother replied, her voice strained.

Roxy knew her mother was looking at her, but Roxy couldn't bring herself to meet her eyes. She knew how much work her mother had put into the gift. But all Roxy could see was that her mother didn't approve of her ambition, her plan for a better life. She was shooting down her daughter's dreams.

"You'll never understand, will you?" Roxy asked.

Sandra pushed herself to her feet. "I understand more than you'll ever know."

Roxy swept her arm around the room. "I'm supposed to be happy here for the rest of my life? Living in a tiny, rundown apartment? Waiting on other people every day?"

Her mother reached for her, but Roxy backed away, stepping out of reach.

"What's wrong with wanting more out of life?" Roxy cried. "What's wrong with wanting to be more than a diner waitress scrounging for tips to pay the rent? What's wrong with wanting to know things? To learn?"

"Nothing," her mother said sharply. "Not as long as you know why you want those things. Don't expect all that knowledge to make you happy, little girl." She gently cupped her hand on Roxy's cheek. "You have to be happy with yourself first. Right here and right now. Or all that book learning won't mean a thing."

Sandra turned and sent a shaky smile to Gina, who was still standing in the middle of the floor, surrounded by popcorn, holding the framed needlework in her hands. "It was nice to see you again, Gina." She placed a kiss on Roxy's cheek. "I love you, sweetie."

Roxy watched her mother leave, too many emotions bouncing around inside her to even think straight. "She doesn't understand." She dropped to her knees and started to pick up the spilled popcorn. Gina placed the picture on the sofa and joined her on the floor. For a few minutes they silently scooped handfuls of greasy popcorn back into the plastic bowl. The conversation with her mother ran over and over again in Roxy's mind.

"Why can't she be proud of me for wanting something more out of life?" But now her mother was disappointed in her and Roxy couldn't shake the deep sadness that washed over her. She slid her legs out in front of her and wiped her hands on her jeans. "She lives for that restaurant. She doesn't know what it's like to want what you don't have."

Gina sat back on her heels. "You think your mother never had hopes and dreams like you?"

Roxy shrugged her shoulders. She'd never really thought about it. "My mother has never talked about her dreams." Then she suddenly remembered that night at the diner not too long ago. Her mother scrubbing dishes and telling her she'd had chances to be selfish, but she didn't let her wants get in the way of Roxy's needs. What dreams did her mother have?

"Are you telling me your mom always wanted to be a single mother, raising a daughter and running a business by herself all at the same time?"

Roxy was ashamed to realize she'd never thought about it before. "No, I'm sure she didn't."

"But she found a way to be happy about it anyway."

"Yeah, I guess she did." Roxy sighed and leaned back against the sofa. Be happy, her mother said. Here and now. But how could she do that? Did she even know how?

Had she been focused on the future for so long now, that she'd forgotten how to enjoy the present? Was that what her mother was saying? To simply do what would make her happy now and not always wait for tomorrow, or the day after, or four years down the road?

What would make her happy? Right here. Right now. Deep brown eyes popped into her brain and instantly, Roxy knew the answer.

Not what...but who.

She'd told herself all along that she couldn't have both Daniel and her education. Was she wrong? Would it possibly work?

Staying away from him hadn't made her think about him any less. And it didn't make her happy. She probably thought about him even more now. He was still a distraction. Why be distracted and unhappy?

She didn't always agree with her mother, but maybe she was right this time. Maybe Roxy did need to do what would make her happy.

Roxy jumped to her feet. "Don't wait up for me."

Gina frowned. "Where are you going?"

She ran into her bedroom and grabbed what she needed from the drawer of the nightstand. "To get some happiness."

Daniel's eyes were burning. He sat slumped at the desk in the chemistry lab and tried to make sense of the symbols swimming on the pages in front of him. He heard the cleaning crew clattering down the hall and knew he should be heading home.

He'd been putting off the next step in his research. Contact with Roxy without benefit of his formula. He should have taken advantage of her surprise visit to his apartment a few days ago, but, coward that he was, he'd slapped some on before he opened the door.

He didn't think he could bear it if she wasn't attracted to him when he wasn't using the elixir.

He missed her fiercely. He understood her concern about being distracted from her studies, but that didn't mean he had to like it. It had been all well and good for him to tell her he'd wait for her to make the next move, but it was driving him crazy. When Cynthia left him, it had barely caused a ripple in his life. He hadn't seen Roxy for three days and the disturbance washed over him in waves.

What if it was a true case of "out of sight, out of mind"? Had the effects of the formula worn off? Did she even think about him any more?

If she didn't contact him soon, he was going to have to arrange a meeting and find out. For scientific purposes, of course.

A knock at the door brought his thoughts back to the lab.

The head of the cleaning crew, a tall woman with skin like worn mahogany, poked her head in the doorway. "Working late again, Professor? I thought you were starting to go home at a decent hour."

"Hey, Mary." Daniel took his glasses off and rubbed his eyes. "Sorry. I'll be out of your way in a minute."

She pushed her cleaning cart into the lab and gave him one of her warm smiles. "That's okay. Take your time."

He shook his head and put his glasses back on. "No, I have to get home before I fall asleep at the wheel."

"Oh, don't even joke about a thing like that, Doctor. I lost my husband, Ernie, that way."

"Really?" Now he felt even worse. "I'm so sorry. What happened?"

She ran a hand through her short gray curls. "He was working late to make a little extra money. Fell asleep on the way home and crashed headlong into a tree. Broke my heart in two. That was twenty years ago and I still miss him every day of my life."

"You've never remarried?"

She shook her head. "Haven't found anyone else with that spark."

"Spark?"

"Oh, don't tell me you've never felt the spark, Doctor. If it's true, that's a sad, sad thing." She pulled up a chair and sat in front of Daniel. "First time I saw my Ernie I felt something special. A connection. An attraction." She shrugged. "You know, a spark."

Daniel thought back to the first time he saw Roxy. It was more like an explosion to his senses than a spark, but definitely an attraction. Definitely special.

"I felt alive when I was around him," Mary went on. "I close my eyes, and I can still feel that spark. Still waiting to feel it again."

The feeling alive part. He could relate to that. He'd missed that feeling in the past few days, the ones without Roxy. How long before she came to him? How long before he felt alive again?

"Don't give up hope, Mary. The guy with the spark may turn out to be right around the next corner."

Mary laughed and stood. "Get out of here so I can do my job."

A bite of winter was in the air as Daniel walked to his car. He turned up the collar on his wool coat and patted the pockets for his gloves. Not there. Damn. Where did he leave them this time?

He found them on the passenger seat, as cold as the icy interior of the car. Blowing on his hands to warm them, he started the engine and sat there for a moment to let it warm up a little before he grasped the cold steering wheel with his gloveless hands.

While he waited for the car to warm up, he looked out the windshield into the darkness. His life had changed so much in the past few days. As sad as it was to admit, he'd never been so focused on another person in his whole life. Not his parents.

Not his friends. Not his students. Not even Cynthia. He'd always been in his own little world, fascinated by his thoughts, his dreams, his imagination.

His experiments.

But somehow, his research was no longer as important to him as Roxy was. How had that happened?

How had he let that happen?

Knowledge was number one. He couldn't forget that. His attraction to Roxy couldn't be allowed to sway him from what was important. He needed to complete his research.

He blew on his hands and rubbed them together. It was time to go home. Time to plan the next steps in this experiment. He couldn't let months of work fall by the wayside for a pretty face and a hot body. He had to see her again and get on with the study.

Daniel put the car into gear and sped out of the parking lot. Roxy was more than a pretty face and a great body. He knew that. She was exuberant and sexy and fun to be with. She was serious about her education and he had to respect her wishes as far as that was concerned. She'd been working her whole life for the benefit of others and she deserved this chance to do something for herself.

But he needed to know how far reaching the effects of the formula were. Did the effects wear off over time? They hadn't worn off for him, but he needed to know how Roxy would feel about him after one day without using the formula. After one week.

There was so much he still needed to know.

He was still arguing back and forth in his mind when he walked into the lobby of his building. As if he had conjured her up in his mind, Roxy sat at the guard's station, holding a hand of cards and laughing with Joe Bartlett.

Did he only *want* to believe that her eyes lit up when she saw him?

"See, Joe, I told you he'd come home sooner or later," she said, speaking to the guard, but looking at Daniel. Her eyes were wide, her smile was wider.

"Thank goodness you're back, Dr. Jennings," Joe said. "This girl is a card shark. She's wiping me out."

"Pennies," Roxy said with a laugh. "We're playing for pennies."

"Who taught you how to play poker?" Daniel asked, rather than asking her what she was doing here, late at night, waiting for him.

"Charlie," she told him, slowly rising to her feet, her gaze still focused on him. "We used to play a lot of poker sitting around the diner. Mom only let me play for toothpicks back then." She placed her cards down on the desk and scooped up a pile of pennies. "Thanks for the game, Joe. It was fun."

"Anytime, Roxy." He nodded to Daniel. "Good night, Dr. Jennings."

"Night, Joe."

Roxy dropped the pennies into the pocket of her coat and then threaded her arm through Daniel's. She hadn't dressed up for him tonight. No makeup. A long red wool coat covered a black sweatshirt and jeans. She smelled like popcorn. She looked beautiful.

He waited until they were in the elevator to ask, "What are you doing here?"

"You said you'd wait for me to make the next move."

He nodded and swallowed because, suddenly, no words would come.

She turned until they were face to face. "Well, I'm moving."

She rubbed against him, making his body grow hard and his breath come faster. Their coats brushed and crackled with static electricity.

Sparks.

Daniel put his hands on her shoulders and looked into her eyes. “Are you sure? Because if we get off this elevator together, you’re not leaving until the morning.”

Her eyes flashed with lights he was certain were for him.

“I know,” she said, her voice clear. “I’m sure.” She brushed her lips along his ear. “I’m ready.”

The bell dinged. The elevator stopped. The door opened. He took her hand and they walked off the elevator together.

Chapter Eight

Her marriage to Todd Morgan had taught Roxy a thing or two. The most important was to take control of her life. To go after what she wanted, because no one else was going to give her anything. She had to reach out and grab what she wanted.

So when Daniel followed her into his dark apartment, Roxy spun around and pinned him against the door as soon as she heard it close behind them. She wanted him. She needed him with every part of her being. Her body had ached for him since the first day she met him, since she first saw him in the deserted chemistry lab. Waiting for him tonight in the lobby just heightened the anticipation that had been building since that day.

She captured his lips with hers, almost desperate in her need for him. Her heart pounded wildly. She'd been imagining this moment for days now. Imagining her arms around him like this, kneading his back. Imagining her lips nibbling his, tasting him, drinking him in.

At this moment she wanted Daniel more than anything. More than a communications degree. More than getting out of the restaurant. At this moment she didn't care about distractions. She only cared about sex and Daniel. Daniel and sex.

She pressed against him, straddling one of his long legs

with hers. She plunged her tongue into his mouth, moaning with desire. They had to get to the bed. She had to touch him. He had to touch her. He had to—

Suddenly, bright lights lit up the wide foyer. She blinked and frowned, breaking the kiss. Leaning back, she looked at Daniel. His hand was still on the light switch.

He looked confused. What was there to be confused about? She thought he wanted the same thing she did. "What?"

"What's going on here?" he asked.

She pulled her arms off his shoulders and stepped away from him. A hot blush crept up the back of her neck. "I thought it was obvious, but if you want me to spell it out..."

He took one of her hands and gently kissed her palm. "No, Roxy, I know you want to make love. There's nothing I'd like more. But there's something else. There's something wrong."

She pulled her hand free and unzipped his jacket. "Nothing's wrong, except we're not in your bed yet."

He chuckled lightly. "We'll get there. Believe me, we'll get there."

She stripped his jacket off him and dropped it to the floor. Then she took his hand and started to pull him down the hall. "Okay, let's go. Show me the way."

Instead of his bedroom, he led her into the living room and to the soft, leather sofa. He sat and brought her down onto the cushions with him. He held her hand between his two warm ones.

"The last I heard from you, you didn't want a man distracting you from your studies."

Right now she didn't want him distracting her from what she wanted. She leaned over and blew in his ear. "Can't I change my mind?"

He groaned low and deep, as if this restraint was costing him dearly. “Of course, but I want to know why.”

She thought guys jumped at the chance to have sex. They were supposed to want to fuck no matter what. Leave it to Daniel to want to talk first. “Why? What does it matter why?” She stroked his muscular thigh with her free hand, starting at his knee and working up. “We agreed the first day we met that we were attracted to each other. Each day we’ve been together we’ve been building on that. I feel like I’m in a pressure cooker.” When she reached his groin, she brushed her hand against his hard arousal. “Daniel, if we don’t have sex soon, I’m going to explode.”

“*You’re* going to explode?”

She smiled and brushed against him again.

He sucked in a deep breath, then cupped her face in his hands and gently kissed her lips. “There’s something else. I thought I picked up a sense of desperation in you tonight, and I was concerned.”

She kissed him back. “I desperately want to have sex with you.”

“You’re sure it’s not something else?”

She smiled and started to unbutton the buttons on the soft gray shirt she’d picked out for him the other day. “Don’t worry about me, Daniel. I’m fine. I want you to fuck me. Fighting it is taking way too much energy.” She kissed him again. Couldn’t he tell how much she needed him? “I’d rather spend my energy in other ways.”

He moaned deep in his throat. When he pushed her coat off her shoulders and down her arms, he didn’t remove it, but left her arms trapped from the elbows down. While her arms were still restrained by the coat, he leaned over and nibbled on her neck. Shivers of awareness rushed along her skin. She struggled against the sleeves holding her hands captive.

He reached behind her and placed his hands over hers. A slow smile spread across his face. “Easy now. We’re not going to rush this. We’re going to take our time. I want our first time to be special.”

She swallowed. “First time?”

“You don’t think once will be enough, do you?”

She shook her head and shivered at the thought.

He lowered his lips back to her throat and nipped her lightly with his teeth. A thrill of excitement ran through her, even as part of her wanted to do it now. Do it right now.

She wasn’t used to this. Wasn’t used to foreplay. Wasn’t used to taking it slow.

She had to fight the urge to rip Daniel’s clothes off and get down to business. She wanted to take control. She wanted to touch him and drive him crazy, instead of the other way around.

Then she realized that this was how she’d always approached sex in the past. She’d been so insecure about not being sexy, about not being attractive, that she used sexual aggressiveness to make sure Todd was satisfied.

She couldn’t remember a single time when Todd was concerned about whether or not she was satisfied. She closed her eyes. Oh God, the last thing she wanted to do right now was think about Todd.

With her eyes closed, she let herself simply feel. Just let herself experience the way Daniel’s hot, wet mouth swept over her throat, leaving a wet trail of tingles in its wake. The way her body throbbed in response to those warm, wet kisses. Her breasts seemed to swell with desire and he hadn’t even touched them yet. Moisture pooled deep within her and dampened her panties.

His hands still held hers down. Her body buzzed. Her nerves thrummed.

Wow, this foreplay stuff wasn't half bad.

He was only touching her with his lips. Only kissing her throat. And still Roxy knew she'd never been loved like this before. And she wanted to love Daniel as she had never loved a man before.

"I want to touch you," she said with a moan. "Let me touch you, Daniel."

He sat back and looked at her, his eyes dark pools of desire. Knowing that he wanted her that much sent a thrill rippling through her. He let go of her hands and helped her shed the coat. She unbuttoned his shirt and slid her hands under the soft fabric. The smooth skin on his shoulders was warm beneath her fingers.

His shirt lay open, exposing his muscular chest and taut abs. She sighed. "You are a sight, Daniel. A welcome sight, at that."

His palms cupped her thighs and she placed her hands on his, trapping him as he had done to her a few moments before. Then she leaned forward and placed light kisses along his collarbone. He dropped his head back to give her better access and she couldn't help but grin. She swept her tongue along his neck. He tasted hot and salty and she was greedy for more.

She trailed wet, open-mouthed kisses down his chest and abdomen. Before this night was over, she would kiss every inch of him. She planned to drive him every bit as crazy as he was making her. His firm abdominal muscles contracted against her lips. His breathing was heavy and ragged. She stopped only when she reached his belt buckle.

The bulging evidence of his arousal stared her in the face.

She put her open mouth on his jeans and breathed hot air onto his crotch. He groaned and shuddered beneath her. Then he jerked his hand free and grabbed the back of her head. She smiled and breathed her heat onto him again.

"Roxy."

Her name was not much more than a moan. She sat up and looked at him. He was beautiful, naked from the waist up. Desire, hot and wild, was written on his face.

He scooped her into his arms and started to stand.

She struggled. "Oh, Daniel, no."

He frowned, but let go of her and sat back down on the sofa. "What? I've been imagining you naked and in my bed for longer than I dare admit."

"Don't try to carry me. I don't want you to hurt yourself."

He rolled his eyes. "I'm not going to hurt myself. I want you in my bed."

"Believe me. I want to be naked and in your bed. Just let me walk with you to the bedroom."

He reached out for her, but instead of scooping her up, he grabbed the hem of her sweatshirt and pulled it over her head. The heated desire on Daniel's face made her actually feel beautiful.

He reached out his hands and touched her breasts lightly through the lacy bra. Her nipples beaded at his touch. He traced a lazy line across her breasts with his finger and she sucked in her breath at the sparks of awareness that shot through her. "Perfect," he murmured as he continued to caress her breasts. "You are perfect."

The retort was on her lips, the words to tell him she knew she was far from perfect. She knew she was too heavy, too round and curvy. But the look on his face, the reverence in his words, told her that he was completely serious. He thought she was perfect just the way she was.

Wow.

She wouldn't have to try so hard to arouse him. She wouldn't have to work at making up for her faults. With Daniel, she could simply be herself.

Roxy took a deep, shaky breath and reached back, releasing the clasp of her bra. She let the straps slide down her arms, baring her breasts for Daniel.

"Oh." The word came out of Daniel's mouth on a ragged sigh.

Roxy smiled, feeling the power she held at that moment. Knowing she made a strong man like Daniel shaky and needy.

But she needed too.

With quick fingers, Roxy unbuckled the belt of his jeans. His cock strained against his zipper. It had to be getting pretty tight in there. It was only right to release him from that constraint. She slowly slid the zipper down and his hard shaft brushed against her hand.

Without taking his eyes off her, he kicked off his shoes and pulled off his socks. Then he stood and she helped him step out of his jeans. A pair of dark gray boxer briefs clung to his body, molding to him perfectly.

"Mmm," she murmured, letting her gaze run over him. "You sure are easy on the eyes, Doc."

He grabbed her by her shoulders and pulled her up to stand in front of him. "My name, damn it," he growled. "Say my name if you're going to make love with me."

"I'm sorry, Daniel." Why had she said that? Was she still trying to keep her distance from him, even now? "I guess I'm more nervous than I thought I'd be."

"Nervous with me?"

She nodded. "Nervous that I'll disappoint you."

He gathered her into his arms and kissed the tip of her nose. "Never."

She rubbed herself lightly against him, brushing her sensitive nipples against the coarse hair on his chest. "I hope not." Todd had never been shy about telling her all the times she had disappointed him.

"So where is the bed you claim to have?" she asked, once again trying to get rid of those annoying thoughts about her ex-husband. Would she never be rid of him?

"So you doubt me?" Daniel asked. He was just the one to totally wipe Todd out of her mind.

"I'm one of those who like to see in order to believe."

He laughed and before she realized what he was doing, he leaned over and scooped her up in his arms. He carried her easily across the living room and down the hall. He pushed open a door that was ajar and flipped on the light switch with his shoulder.

"Hey, you do have a bed," Roxy said. It looked extra wide and extra long, or maybe it just seemed that way from her vantage point up here in Daniel's arms. The walls were beige. The black comforter on the bed stood out in sharp contrast. The bed seemed to take up most of the room. In only two steps, they'd reached it. But she remained in Daniel's arms.

She squirmed a little. "You can put me down now."

He held her a bit closer and nibbled on her ear. "I don't know if I will," he said, the warmth of his breath washing over her neck. "I like holding you."

"I'm too heavy."

"Stop worrying about it. You're not too heavy," he replied,

but he set her gently down onto the bed. He knelt down and untied her sneakers. Then he stripped her socks from her feet. He caressed her feet with his hands. Oh God, that felt wonderful. “You have very pretty feet.”

“No one has pretty feet,” she said. She tried to pull her feet away, but he held on.

“Why do you want to argue with me tonight?” He rubbed the balls of her feet with his thumbs and she thought she might melt, it felt so good. “You have pretty feet.”

“Thank you,” she said because she didn’t know what else to say. She wasn’t used to compliments, especially about her weight and feet.

“Stand up,” he said. “Let’s get these jeans off you.”

“Okay.”

She stood and reached for the snap, but his fingers beat her to it. After the snap, he lowered the zipper and pushed the denim over her hips. He hooked her damp panties with his thumbs and they ended up on the floor along with the jeans. She held onto his shoulders as she stepped out of them.

“Beautiful,” he murmured as he ran his gaze over her. And before she had a chance to respond, he placed a finger on her lips. “Beautiful,” he repeated.

She couldn’t help smiling. If nothing else, Daniel had given her a feeling of worth. He made her feel beautiful. Desirable.

But she wanted so much more.

She swept her hands down his sides, skimming his ribs, catching the waistband of his boxer briefs with her fingers. She caught his amused gaze. “It’s only fair.”

He spread his arms wide. “Be my guest.”

She slid the soft cotton down over his hips and his heavy cock. The briefs landed at his feet and he stepped out of them.

And finally he stood before her in all his glory. His long, muscular legs she wanted tangled with hers. His taut buns she wanted to touch with her trembling fingers. His magnificent arousal she wanted to take into her eager body.

She was amazed that she stood naked before him and felt confident and sexy and powerful. How did he do that to her? Or did she do it for herself?

Or maybe the two of them made the right combination. In the back of her mind, a voice told her she should be upset with that thought, but at the moment she didn't know why.

"Lay back on my bed," Daniel said softly. "Fulfill my fantasy."

She spread her arms out and fell backward, her body cushioned by the soft mattress and silky comforter beneath her. She slid back on the bed, until her head sank into the soft pillow. Her eyes never left Daniel's. He was gazing at her as if she were the most precious thing on Earth and she could almost believe it.

"I've pictured you like this," he told her. "No, not exactly like this. My imagination never came up with anything as wonderful as you are right now."

Her breath caught in her throat. No words would come, at least words he would want to hear, so she bit her tongue and smiled.

He took off his glasses and set them on the nightstand before he joined her on the bed. His weight on the mattress sent her rolling toward him and she wrapped her arms around him. He stretched out beside her, the heat from his body warming her through and through. When he leaned over to suckle at her breast, she suddenly sat up.

How could she have forgotten the most important thing of all? "Wait a minute."

He frowned. “What?”

“Be right back.”

She jumped off the bed. Where did she leave her coat? She ran out of the bedroom. It was lying in a mound on the sofa. She turned it upside down, trying to get her hand in the right pocket. Pennies flew everywhere, but she left her poker winnings where they lay. Finally she found what she was looking for and turned back to the bedroom.

“What’s the matter?” Daniel stood in the doorway. “Are you all right?”

She smiled and sauntered past him into the bedroom. “Oh, yeah.”

He followed her back into the bedroom. “Roxy?”

She dropped a handful of colorful condom packages onto the mattress. “I came prepared.”

He laughed and grabbed her around the waist. They fell as one onto the bed. Skin rubbed against skin, hot and smooth. Legs tangled together, long and strong. Their lips met and brushed and sucked.

“Now, where was I?” he asked after a moment.

Finally he captured one aching breast in his mouth and Roxy moaned out loud. “Oh, yeah. That’s so good.”

He suckled harder, sending pinpricks of sensations flowing from the sensitive nipple to all parts of her body. She dove her fingers into his hair and held his head in place. He could do that forever as far as she was concerned.

He stroked her thigh with his long fingers. Higher and higher with each caress. Shivers danced along her skin. She closed her eyes and simply experienced the marvelous sensations. The unexpected feeling of being cherished. Of being cared for. Of being incredibly aroused.

One of his fingers dipped into the moisture between her legs. As he skimmed her most sensitive spot, Roxy arched her back, pushing harder against him.

The many sensations whirling around her threatened to overwhelm her. Could any one person feel so much at one time and not come apart? Not go crazy with need? Roxy had come close, but she'd never reached the pinnacle of satisfaction before. But as he continued to stroke and suck, the threads of desire wound tighter and tighter within her, until suddenly they burst into a fireworks of sensations.

She gasped at the force of the climax. Her body bucked and her breath came in heavy pants. She closed her eyes and let the waves carry her away until they slowly subsided and left her on the bed again with Daniel.

When she opened her eyes, he was sitting up beside her. Hot desire was still clear in his expression, but there was a caring look on his face as well. She smiled. "Wow."

Her eyes filled with tears at the thought that Daniel had cared enough to see that she was satisfied, even before he was. She sat up and closed her fingers around a condom packet. She'd be happy to return the favor.

Were those tears in her eyes? Daniel was about to ask her if she was all right when she smiled and grabbed one of the colorful packets strewn across the mattress. He remained silent as he watched her rip the condom packet open and fling the plastic aside. She wore a smug smile when she pushed his chest and he fell onto his back on the mattress.

She knelt beside him. "Hmm, let's see. How does this work?"

He sucked in his breath as she rubbed the edge of the condom against his erection. She stroked the length of him and he moaned deep in his throat.

"Hmm. Wait a minute," she said, with a touch of humor in her voice.

"What?" He started to sit up, but she placed her hand on his chest and pushed him back down onto the mattress.

"Don't worry about a thing." Her voice was soft and seductive. "You just lie there and enjoy. I'll take care of you."

Then she bent over him and covered his aching cock with her hot, wet mouth. Oh, God. He sucked in his breath as she took him in deep, so deep. Was that the back of her throat? Oh, God.

He closed his eyes as she rode him with her mouth. Sparks zapped through his system as she surrounded him with her wet heat. Pressure began to build, swirling down through him, focusing every sensation to his cock. How long would he be able to enjoy this before he lost control?

Then she released him and began to run her tongue from base to tip and back again. He closed his eyes and moaned.

"Oh, you like that?" she asked, her voice a soft purr. She stroked him again with her long fingers and he struggled to maintain control. "You taste so good. I could do that all night long."

"Not tonight," he groaned. "I want to be inside you when I come."

"Getting close, huh?"

"Oh, yeah. Real close."

"Okay. Let's see what we can do." Slowly, she rolled the condom over him, using long, hard strokes that threatened to send him over the edge. Then his eyes flew open when she moved over him. Straddling him, she sank down, taking him into her warm, ready body.

He grabbed her waist and plunged into her wet softness. Finally. "Roxy, my God."

Her eyes were on fire. The smile on her face lit up the room. She moved over him, one moment burying him deep within her, the next moment almost letting him go.

Her beautiful breasts bounced with her movements. Her blonde hair flew around her face like a wild halo. Her arms were stretched out to her sides. She rode him as if he was a bucking bronco. He could watch her like that for hours.

He didn't have hours. He grasped her by the hips and matched her raucous rhythm, moving his hips in time with hers. His body buzzed with the tension building within him.

The air was charged with electricity. Sparks could have flown around them and he wouldn't have been surprised. What was this energy that pulsed in the air around them? What was it that emanated from her as if it was a part of her being? What was it that she brought out in him that no one else ever had?

The sparks built within him. They ignited. Exploded. He shattered in the fireworks and he knew what it was.

Passion. Daniel had found his passion.

Chapter Nine

He had to tell her about the potion.

Daniel's stomach clenched at the thought and the marvelous feeling of euphoria evaporated. Roxy lay beside him, snuggled against his shoulder, her soft hair brushing his face. He kissed the top of her head and she nestled even closer against him. Her eyes were closed but her hand made lazy circles across his hip. No wonder she was tired. She put her all into love-making, the same as she did everything else.

His body immediately responded to her leg wrapped around him. To her gentle caresses. To the memories of her hands upon him. The sparks they generated together.

Her hand crept lower. Her fingers brushed against his hardening cock.

"Hello," she murmured. She took his fullness in her hand and started to stroke.

He moaned. He wanted nothing more than to roll on top of her and gaze at her beautiful face while he buried himself in her soft body. But how could he make love to her again when he knew he had been manipulating her emotions from the very beginning?

Jolts of desire coursed through him as Roxy continued to stroke and knead his most sensitive flesh. He groaned and his hand went instinctively to her full breast. He knew he should pull it away, but his hand wouldn't leave. His fingers gently squeezed her nipple instead.

His body seemed to be overriding his brain. He'd picked a most inconvenient time to get a conscience.

Roxy rolled on top of him. Her soft skin slid against his. Her luscious breasts rubbed against his chest. She straddled him and rained hot, wet kisses along his throat.

"Roxy…"

When she silenced him with that incredible mouth, he forgot what he was going to say. All rational thought flew from his brain.

He wrapped his arms around her and rolled them over, so he was lying on top of her. He pushed himself up to his knees so that he could gaze down at her. After he skimmed her ribs with his fingers, he scooped up her generous breasts with his tingling palms.

He lowered his mouth and sucked one taut nipple into his mouth. Roxy gasped and arched her back. She grabbed his shoulders with her fingers and dug in, scraping his skin lightly with her nails.

"Yes," she cried. "More, Daniel, more."

He chuckled and sucked harder. He teased the sensitive nipple with his tongue, then grazed it lightly with his teeth. She gasped again and rocked beneath him. His cock became even harder, knowing he was unleashing the passion in her as she was unleashing it in him.

His blood pounded in his head. His breaths came in loud gasps. At first he thought the ringing he heard was only in his ears. But then he realized it was the phone on the desk on the other side of the room. Roxy stilled beneath him.

"Who would be calling this late?" he wondered out loud. He

wasn't leaving his comfortable position to get up and answer it. He'd let the machine pick it up.

"Dr. Jennings?" a familiar female voice, slightly shaky, spoke into the answering machine. "It's Gina Manetti. I'm looking for Roxy. If you see her, could you have her call me right away? Her mother's been taken to the hospital."

Roxy scrambled out from under him. She bounded across the room and picked up the receiver. "Gina?"

Daniel grabbed his glasses and then watched Roxy as she listened to Gina. When she started to shake, he pulled a blanket off the bed. As he wrapped it around her, she looked at him with wide eyes full of fear.

"Okay, I'm going right to the hospital," Roxy said to Gina. "She was still breathing when the ambulance got there, right? She was still conscious?" She sank onto the desk chair. "Oh, God."

Daniel rushed to gather up their clothing. In a testament to their passion, the various items were strewn in a path from the bedroom to the living room. By the time he got back to the bedroom with all of their clothes, Roxy had hung up the telephone.

He dumped the clothes on the bed and rushed over to her. She stood and he wrapped his arms around her. He could feel her trembling. He rubbed her back and wished he could do something to help her.

"Are you all right?" he asked. Stupid question.

Roxy shook her head and stepped out of his embrace. "I have to get to the hospital. My mom collapsed and was taken to the emergency room."

She threaded her arms through her bra straps, but her hands were shaking too much to hook it. Daniel stepped around behind her and did it for her. She tearfully smiled her thanks and threw on the rest of her clothes.

Daniel dressed quickly. "I'll drive."

"You don't have to do that," she told him as she tied her sneakers. "I'll take a cab."

"I want to," he told her. He grabbed his keys off the dresser. "I don't want you to have to go there all by yourself."

"I'm perfectly capable of doing this myself." She turned away from him, picked up her badly rumpled coat off the sofa and shook it out. A few pennies flew out and joined those already strewn across the floor.

Why had her voice gotten so cool all of a sudden? What happened to the warm, passionate woman who had been in his arms only minutes ago?

"I know you *can*," he said carefully. He picked up his coat from where it still lay in a pile by the front door. "But that's no reason why you should have to."

"Daniel, my mother and I both had to learn how to deal with what life throws us without relying on a man." Her hands were still shaking as she buttoned up the coat. "You and I had great sex, but I don't need you holding my hand to cross the street."

Great sex? Was that all it was? He knew she was upset, but the comment still stung.

Daniel pushed the hurt away. She wasn't thinking clearly at the moment. "This is not the time for a stupid argument. You can wait for a cab or we could be on our way right now, if you'd simply let me drive you."

She opened her mouth as if she was going to shoot out another comeback, but then she closed it again. She nodded. "You're right. Let's go."

Roxy didn't say anything on the elevator ride to the lobby,

or on the quick walk to the car. After she'd settled into her seat, she sighed and let her head fall back against the headrest. She didn't speak until Daniel pulled out onto the street.

"She tried to find me."

The roads were practically deserted. Daniel turned a corner and then glanced at Roxy. "What?"

"When she started to feel bad. She tried to call me. I guess Gina went out after I left, so Mom left a message on the machine. She might have been able to get help faster if I'd been home."

"Oh, no," Daniel said sharply. "You're not going to let yourself feel guilty because you were with me."

Her voice quivered. "But she couldn't find me. I could have gotten her help."

"She's a grown woman. She knows how to dial 911."

"But what if she was too sick to dial the phone?"

"Then she wouldn't have been able to call you, either."

"Oh, yeah, you're right." Roxy let out a shaky laugh. "I guess I'm not thinking straight."

"So who did she call?"

"Charlie. He came right over and called 911."

"Which gets us back to why she didn't call them to begin with."

Roxy shrugged. "I'm going to ask her that myself, but I think I know what she'll tell me."

They were almost there. He pulled into the parking ramp. "What?"

"She hates doctors."

"Doesn't sound like she was thinking very clearly either."

"Well, no," Roxy said wryly. "She was lying on the floor

having trouble breathing." A sob escaped her. "Oh, God."

"We'll be there in a minute," Daniel said. "I'm sure she's in the best of hands." He pulled into a parking space in the ramp. Roxy was out the door before he even had the chance to shift into park.

Roxy stood on trembling legs, impatiently waiting for the elevator, when Daniel came up beside her. She didn't want to be grateful he was here, but she was. She didn't want to depend on any man again, not even Daniel. Not after all she'd been through with Todd. Yet here she was, glad Daniel was with her.

It was one thing to like him, to spend time with him. To have sex even.

But it was quite another thing for him to be coming with her to the hospital in the middle of the night. To talk her through her panic and offer words of encouragement. To simply stand beside her waiting for the elevator that was taking an eternity to come.

She didn't want to become dependant on him. It would be too easy to do just that. But when he slid his hand into hers, she didn't pull away. She needed the contact right now like she needed air to breathe. She even returned the little squeeze of encouragement.

Finally the elevator doors slid open and they were on their way to the emergency room. When they stepped off the elevator, Roxy's stomach twisted. The odor of disinfectant in the air didn't help much. In fact, it was almost her undoing.

She grasped Daniel's hand like a lifeline and took a few deep breaths.

He stopped in the middle of the hall and looked at her with a frown. "Are you all right?"

She nodded and took another deep breath.

"You're not going to pass out on me, are you?"

"No." She took another breath. "I don't even think I'm going to throw up."

He drew back and stared at her. "I didn't know that was an option."

"Oh, yeah. But I think I'm over the urge."

"Glad to hear it."

She found herself smiling. "I'm glad you're here, Daniel."

"Glad I could be here."

They were ushered quickly into the room where her mother lay, hooked up to what seemed to be a million wires and machines. Roxy rushed to her mother's side. She tried not to show her fear, but Roxy didn't know how well she hid it on her face.

Her mother looked up at her with wide eyes. Roxy's eyes filled with tears.

"Don't cry, little girl," her mother said softly. "I'll be okay."

"What happened?"

"They think she had a heart attack."

Roxy turned at the sound of the voice. She hadn't noticed that Charlie was there too. But of course he would be.

"Heart attack?" She remembered how her mother had struggled to breathe when she'd come to the apartment to see her. Climbing all those steps. Having her daughter yell at her. Throwing her words back in her face. Did that have something to so with her collapse?

"They're monitoring her now," Charlie told her. "They'll be running some more tests pretty soon. Then they can tell for sure."

Roxy grasped her mother's cool, clammy hand. She wondered how she could ever let go of it again. How could she ever make it up to her?

Her mother glanced over her shoulder. "You brought your own doctor with you?"

Daniel stepped up to the bed. "At the moment I'm sorry I'm not a cardiologist. How are you feeling, Mrs. Erickson?"

"It's Sandy," she said, "and I feel like I've been beat up, that's how I feel."

"Mom, I'm so sorry about the picture," Roxy cried. "It's a beautiful picture and you worked so hard on it and I'm going to hang it up in the living room and look at it every day."

"It's all right, Roxy. I know it wasn't what you wanted."

"No, Mom. It was beautiful. I'm so sorry I yelled at you. Maybe if I hadn't upset you so much, this wouldn't have happened."

Her mother shook her head. "That pitiful little argument? That was nothing compared to the way you used to yell at me when you were a teenager. Remember some of the shouting matches we used to have?"

Roxy nodded, but she didn't believe for one minute that the confrontation at her apartment had nothing to do with her mother's attack. It probably started it. She'd fought with her mother and went off to fall in bed with a sexy man and then her mother couldn't find her when she needed her most. Some daughter she was.

"I'm sorry," she said, her voice sounding raspy.

"It's okay, little girl, but I need you to do something for me."

"Of course, anything."

"They're not going to let me out of here in time to open for breakfast. I'll need you to run the restaurant for me, at least for today."

Just for today? Roxy took in her mother's labored breathing, her gray complexion, and knew she would be away from the restaurant for more than one day.

"Maybe you could close the diner for a day or two," Charlie suggested. "Everyone will understand."

"I can't afford to close down," her mother moaned. One of the monitors responded shrilly to her distress. She weakly squeezed Roxy's hand. "You have to keep it open."

"I can do it. No problem," Roxy said. Her class schedule flew through her head. No exams this week. That was a good thing. She'd get in touch with her professors and let them know what happened. She could get the assignments and keep up on her work for a couple days.

A nurse walked into the examining room and frowned. She pushed Roxy out of the way and checked the screens of the monitors surrounding her mother. She turned to look at Roxy and then glanced at Charlie and Daniel as well. "I think you've disturbed my patient enough. You'll all have to go out to the waiting room now. The doctor will be out to talk to you shortly."

Daniel nodded and put his arm around Roxy's shoulder. She glanced back at her mother. Roxy recognized the fear in her mother's eyes. It burned a hole in Roxy's stomach. She crossed her arms in front of herself to hold in the pain. She managed a weak smile for her mother before she let Daniel lead her out into the bright hallway.

Daniel wished there was something he could do for Roxy. She looked like a frightened little girl, curled up in a chair in the far corner of the waiting room. She didn't seem to want either Daniel or Charlie with her. Leave it to Roxy to want to suffer alone.

Charlie paced the room for a while, and then he came over and sat next to Daniel. They both looked across the room at Roxy for a moment, but she didn't acknowledge them.

"She looks lost," Daniel said softly.

"Sure she is," Charlie replied. "It's been Sandy and Roxy against the world since the day Roxy was born."

"What happened to Roxy's father?"

"Jim was a friend of mine," Charlie said, lowering his voice further. "Good friend. Lousy husband. Fancied himself a lady's man. He should've never married her." Charlie shook his head. "Took off as soon as Sandy told him she was pregnant. Damn fool. He took off and we never heard from him again. Good riddance, I say. He didn't deserve them."

"Why do I get the impression you would have liked to have taken his place?" Daniel asked.

"I would have done it in a heartbeat," Charlie said. He turned to stare at the emergency room door. "In a heartbeat."

"Why didn't you?"

"It wasn't for lack of trying. But Sandy, once she got burned, she wasn't going to trust a man again." He picked up a magazine and flipped through the pages for a moment. Then he looked over at Daniel, pain etched in his weathered features. "Once she found out she could do okay on her own, the fool woman decided she didn't need a man."

"So you've been waiting for her all this time?"

Charlie shrugged and tossed the magazine back on the table beside him. "Don't have anyplace else to go."

Daniel nodded. He was quiet for a moment and then asked the question he'd been dying to ask. "What's Roxy's story?"

Charlie flashed him a knowing smile. "Yeah, those women sure had bad judgment in men. Todd Morgan was too much like

Jim Erickson for my taste, but what can you tell a teenage girl in love? Sandy tried to warn her, but the girl had to learn for herself the hard way. At least Todd didn't take off like Jim did, but he might as well have for the pitiful amount of attention he gave that girl."

"He used her," Daniel said, remembering what Roxy had told him.

"Well, it pains me to say it, but she let herself be used. She could have thrown him out on his ass once he made it clear he wasn't committed to her or their marriage, but she stuck around, probably hoping he'd change."

Daniel looked at Roxy sitting across the room. She was staring straight ahead, her arms wrapped around her middle. She shouldn't have to try to comfort herself. He rose and crossed the room.

Her bottom lip quivered. "I'm scared, Daniel. What if something happens to my mom?"

Daniel sat beside her. "They're going to take good care of her." He put his arm around her and she dropped her head onto his shoulder.

"Thank you for being here," she whispered.

"And yet you didn't want me to come."

She shook her head, but didn't say anything more. He wished he knew what was going on in that stubborn head of hers.

"Why not, Roxy? Why didn't you want me here?"

"I don't want to lean on someone else." As if to prove her point, she sat up and left his shoulder cold and empty. "I've become so much stronger since Todd left. I don't want to be weak like that ever again."

"It's not weak to seek comfort when you're hurt or scared.

It's human." He took her hand. "Besides, that's what friends are for."

She shrugged and looked around them. "I wish the doctor would come out. All this waiting is driving me crazy."

Charlie was pacing again and Daniel watched Roxy follow him with her eyes.

"He loves you very much," Daniel said.

"I love him too," Roxy told him, her eyes still following Charlie around the waiting room. "He's the closest thing to a dad I ever had. I know he loves my mom, but she says she won't ever get married again."

"Will you?" He didn't know those words were going to come out of his mouth until they were gone. Then it was too late.

Roxy swung her gaze back around to Daniel. She pulled her hand away. "Will I what?"

"Ever get married again?" He said the words lightly, but he studied her carefully.

"Well, I'll never say never like my mom," Roxy said slowly. She glanced at Daniel, but then slid her gaze away. "But, um, I can't even think about it for years. I'm not even dating until after I get my degree, remember?"

"I remember," Daniel said. His temper flared. He was so sick of hearing her say that. "You won't date, but you'll jump into bed with me."

Roxy's eyes widened and she backed away from him. "I didn't see you turning me away."

Daniel put his hand on her arm, before she could walk away. "I'm not the one who said I wasn't going to get involved with anyone." He slid his hand up her arm, remembering the feel of her skin against his not long ago. "I'm the one who said I wanted to find passion." She stared at him. Her beautiful breasts rose and fell as she took several deep breaths. She opened her mouth, but he never found out if she was going to agree that making love with him was wonderful or if she was going to demand that he take his hands off her.

The emergency room door opened and the doctor walked into the room.

Chapter Ten

"She'll be in cardiac care for at least a couple more days," Roxy repeated to yet another concerned customer for the millionth time that day. "The doctor says he's real optimistic about her recovery. I don't know how long it will be before she can come back to work."

She nodded and smiled as the woman gave her best wishes for her mother's recovery. Roxy knew her mother was well-known in the community, but she'd never realized how many people knew and cared about her mom. It gave her a warm feeling inside.

Roxy was still worried, but she couldn't help but wonder when her mother would be able to come back to work. How long was she going to have to miss school to manage the restaurant? When would she ever get time to catch up on her schoolwork?

No sense worrying about it right now. Right now she just wanted to get through the rest of the evening before she collapsed from exhaustion.

Roxy turned her concentration back to the shift schedule she was working on. Her feet hurt, her hair smelled like grease, and she desperately wanted to go home, but that didn't look like it was going to happen for a while yet.

How did her mother do it?

Well, for one thing, her mother probably routinely got a

good night's sleep before she put in fourteen hours at the restaurant. Roxy had never gotten around to sleeping in Daniel's bed, or anywhere else, last night.

Daniel.

Just thinking his name made her want to sigh. What was she going to do about him? And what was that remark about getting married? Was he just trying to get her mind off her mother's attack, or had he been serious?

She probably didn't want to know.

She did know she didn't want to get married again. Not now. Maybe not ever. She wasn't going to cater to a man's whims ever again.

Not even when they had to do with a big, soft bed and kisses to die for.

She had to stop thinking about Daniel and his kisses. She had to figure out how to cover all the shifts until her mother could start working again.

"Roxy, I'm going to start sweeping up," Amy said from behind her.

Roxy looked up from the schedule and noticed that the restaurant was almost empty. Thank goodness it was nearly closing time. She smiled at Amy. "Thanks. Um, wait a sec. Do you think you'd be able to work a couple extra hours a day for the next few days? If everyone can do that, we should be able to cover everything okay."

Amy nodded. "If my sitter can come early. I'll let you know."

"Thanks."

Roxy heard the door open and somehow she knew it was him. Tall and handsome, sexier than a man had a right to be. He had a smile on his face that she knew was meant only for her. Her heart leapt at the sight of him. She didn't want it to, but there it was. She had a leaping heart and it was all because of Daniel.

He sat at the counter beside her and kissed her cheek. "How's it going?"

"Okay. Mom's resting comfortably."

He reached over and started rubbing her shoulders. "How about you?"

Oh, God, but his fingers were like heaven as they kneaded her tight muscles. "Me? Um, well, resting sounds wonderful. Sleep sounds even better."

"Let me take you home. I stopped by to see if you wanted a ride."

"I'd love it, but I need to help close up."

Amy was sweeping behind the counter and must have overheard. "We're almost done," she told Roxy. "You go ahead. You've been here since six this morning. We can close."

Boy, it was tempting. Just the thought of crawling into her warm bed had her nearly melting on the stool. "Are you sure?"

Amy laughed. "Go on. Paulie and Ralph are still here. We'll be fine. Let the handsome man take care of you."

Wait. Didn't she want to take care of herself? But Roxy didn't protest when Daniel took her hand and helped her up from the stool. She was too tired.

Her legs felt unsteady. She was certain it was the weariness, and not the man, that caused her knees to be weak. Somehow, now that they'd made love, she looked at Daniel a little differently. The fingers that slid across her palm just now had cupped her naked breasts last night. The lips that smiled at her had nibbled on her skin.

And her body remembered vividly the way he'd made her feel. And now that he was close to her again, now that she could pick up his unique scent and see his warm eyes, she wanted to touch him again. Wanted to feel his skin beneath her palms. To tangle legs and tongues. To mingle their breath and meld their bodies.

But she was so damn tired.

Daniel helped her into her coat and led her out the door. The cold blast of air didn't revive her like it sometimes did. She even let him open the car door for her. She rested her head back and closed her eyes before he'd even climbed in the other side.

She didn't remember the short ride to her apartment. He woke her up with a soft kiss on her lips. She wrapped her arms around his neck and returned the kiss. She drew strength from him and didn't stop to wonder whether or not that was a good thing. It was what she needed at the moment and she wasn't going to question it.

"Come up with me," she said.

"Are you sure?" he asked. "You look exhausted."

She nodded. "I am. But I still want you to come with me." She rubbed her cheek against his. "Come on, Daniel. Spend the night with me."

"I'm not sure that's such a good idea."

She brushed her lips over his. "It's a wonderful idea."

He chuckled lightly and his warm breath blew over her cheek, sending light shivers skittering across her skin. "Well, it would be if you were awake."

"I'm awake enough to know I want you."

"Hold on. I'll be right there." He got out of the car and came around to open her door. She'd never waited for a man to open the door for her, but somehow she couldn't summon the energy to even pull on the handle. Maybe Daniel was right. But when he held out his hand, her body tingled as she slid her palm over his.

She caught her heel stepping out of the car and, if Daniel hadn't caught her, she would have landed face-first on the pavement.

He drew her up along his hard body so that they were plastered against each other, face to face. Wow. She melted against him. She wanted more of that body-to-body action. Just because the stupid heel of her shoe got caught on the car didn't mean she couldn't maneuver other parts of her body to their best advantage.

"Come up with me." She rubbed her lips against his and longed for more.

"I'll come up and help you get ready for bed." He stepped away and put his arm around her waist. "I think you're practically asleep on your feet."

"I'm okay, really," she said, but her exhausted body didn't play along. The libido was willing, but her body wimped out on her again. She tripped over her feet again going up the walk. Damn, she didn't want to turn into a weak, needy woman.

Daniel put his arm around her and helped her the rest of the way up the walk. She didn't like it much, and wanted to pull away to prove she didn't need to lean on him, but she was actually afraid she'd trip again and that would be even worse.

"Wait," Daniel said, stopping at the bottom of the stairs. "I'm going to carry you up the stairs."

"You will not!" Roxy looked up the long, steep stairs, horrified. "Just what we need, you stumbling and both of us falling down the stairs." She started to stomp away from him, but Daniel grabbed her arm.

The door to the lower apartment opened and Mr. Campbell stepped out, a frown on his face, his bony chest pushed out in macho protector mode. “Are you okay, Roxy?” He glanced from her to Daniel and back again. “Do you need some help?”

She cleared her throat. “I’m fine. Really. This is my friend, Daniel Jennings. Daniel, this is my landlord, Hiram Campbell.”

They shook hands, Mr. Campbell still sizing Daniel up. Daniel stepped to her side as if claiming her. Men.

“Daniel thinks I need help climbing my own stairs. Like I haven’t done it myself for years.” Roxy rolled her eyes for effect. Then ruined it by yawning so hard her body shook.

“You’re tired,” Mr. Campbell said, somehow ending up on the other side of her. “You work too hard. How’s your mother?”

“She’s doing better, thanks.” She yawned again. She couldn’t help herself. “How’s Mabel?”

“Well, Roxy, she’ll tell you she’s fine, but the truth is her hip’s been bothering her. She needs a replacement, but the thought of surgery scares her.”

Roxy nodded. “I can understand that. But if there’s anything I can do to help out, you let me know.”

He nodded. “Thank you. But I think you have enough to do already. Did you work all day?” Mr. Campbell took one of her arms and Daniel took the other and somehow they were both walking her up the steps. “You shouldn’t work all day and all night, too. That’s not good for anyone, Roxy.”

“I like your landlord,” Daniel said. “He’s a smart man.”

“Oh, shut up,” she snapped, but her heart wasn’t in it. In fact, warmth rushed through her that had nothing to do with being crushed between the two men as they shuffled up the stairs.

They finally reached the upper landing and she pulled away from them. “Thanks, guys. Really. I’m okay.” She fumbled for her key and then couldn’t seem to get it in the stupid keyhole.

Why was life conspiring against her tonight?

Daniel gently took the key out of her hand and slid it in the lock. Mr. Campbell slapped him on the back as if they were now good buddies and dropped a kiss on her cheek. "Good night, now. You take care of yourself." And he disappeared down the stairs.

"Nice guy," Daniel said, pushing her door open. "Let's get you inside."

Just then she realized that Daniel had never seen her apartment before. It was so not like his apartment. No bank of windows overlooking the city. No elegant furniture. No spacious rooms.

What would he think of the ugly, mismatched furniture? The dingy walls? The tiny rooms? Why did she ask him up here? She had to send him home right now. Sex would just have to wait.

She turned around to push him back out onto the landing, but found herself in his arms instead. Daniel lowered his lips to hers and gave her what had to be the softest, sweetest kiss in the history of kisses. She sank against him, drinking him in, savoring the feel of him. Letting him support all her weight as they entered the apartment and closed the door behind them.

Much too soon, he lifted his head. But his smile was enough to start the tickles in her stomach again. "Where's your bedroom?"

Okay, so maybe she didn't want to wait on the sex. This was her home, for better or worse. If Daniel had sex on the brain too, maybe he wouldn't notice the apartment. She took his hand and started to lead the way.

"Is Gina home?"

"Hey, Gina!" Roxy called out. After there was no reply, she said, "Guess not. She's been going out on a lot of dates lately. A lot of first dates." She shrugged her shoulder and headed for her bedroom with Daniel in tow.

She glanced around quickly after she flicked on the light. Thank goodness she'd taken the time to make her bed the last time she was here. When was that? It seemed like forever. She saw there were only a few pieces of clothing strewn around. It could have been much worse.

In fact, now that Daniel was actually in her bedroom, she thought things were pretty darn good.

Well, her mother was in the hospital, that wasn't good. She had to miss classes to manage the restaurant, that wasn't so good either. And she was so tired she couldn't see straight.

Her knees wobbled a little as she turned around to face him. Daniel reached out and caught her before she could fall. He gathered her into his arms and kissed her cheek.

She sighed. Yeah, all and all, things were pretty darn good.

Daniel felt the warm breath from Roxy's sigh brush against his face. He wished there were more he could do for her, but putting her to bed was the only thing he could think of. Having had a taste of the passion she held inside that luscious body of hers, he was anxious to try it again. But tonight was not the time.

"Here, I think you should sit down."

She didn't resist as Daniel backed her up to her bed and sat her down on the edge of the mattress atop a blue-flowered comforter. Her eyes were half-closed. She lifted her hands to start unbuttoning her white shirt.

Daniel closed his hands over hers and pushed her shaky hands into her lap. "Let me."

She frowned. "I... I can do it."

"I know you can," he said softly, "but why don't you let me do it for you?"

"Why?" she asked, sleepily.

"Because I want to do this for you."

"Oh." A small smile lifted her lips. "Okay."

Daniel sat beside her on the bed. He took his time slipping each pearly button through its buttonhole. As the shirt loosened, it fell open. Tantalizing inches of her soft skin were revealed with each button. He couldn't resist pressing his lips to the base of her throat. Her pulse beat wildly against his lips. His cock came alive, rising to attention in his pants.

Once the shirt was completely unbuttoned, Daniel slid it off one smooth shoulder, brushing her skin with his hand as he pushed the fabric down her arm. Then he repeated the process with her other shoulder and slid his hand down her other arm as well.

The arms of the shirt wouldn't go over her hands and it took him a moment to realize that there were buttons on the cuffs. Of course, there were. He lifted one of her hands to his lips and kissed her palm as he unbuttoned the cuff and then let the shirt slide off her arm. She was watching him intently as he kissed the other palm before he removed her shirt completely.

His breath caught as he gazed at the white lacy bra that cupped her two perfect breasts. Though he itched to rip the bra from her body and gather their fullness into his hands, he knew he couldn't indulge in that yearning right now. He was simply undressing her. Tonight was for Roxy.

He knelt down on the floor in front of her, shifting a little to relieve the pressure in his trousers. He unlaced both of her shoes and slipped them from her feet. He peeled the short white socks off and placed one of her bare feet in his lap. With strong strokes, he began to massage her. He knew her feet had to hurt, she'd been on them all day. The moan of pleasure she made brought a smile to his lips.

After he rubbed her other foot, he rose on his knees. He looked at Roxy. Her eyes were closed. "Roxy? Can you stand up for a minute?"

She nodded silently. She was a little shaky, but Daniel placed his hands on her legs to steady her. He unbuckled her belt and pulled it out of the loops. It joined her shirt on the little wooden chair in the corner.

He unbuttoned the waistband of her black slacks and then swallowed before he lightly touched the zipper. His hand trembled slightly as he pulled it down. The raspy noise sounded loud in the silence surrounding them.

Her eyes were closed again. But he knew she wasn't sleeping. He could tell she was taking deep breaths from the way her chest was moving. And her legs were trembling.

Enough of this. He grasped the slacks and slid them down her legs. They rustled as they fell and hit the floor.

"Honey, you have to help me now," he said softly. "Step out of these, okay?"

Silently, she lifted each foot as he touched it and soon the pants joined the shirt and belt on the chair.

She stood before him and he could barely catch his breath. She had a body made for sex and she wore only a lacy bra and panties. And a smile. Her eyes were open and she looked at him with blatant desire.

His hands itched with the need to touch her. His blood pulsed with his craving for her. His cock ached with the desire to sink into her soft body.

She held out her arms and he couldn't resist her any longer. He rose to his feet and took her into his arms. Her mouth was hot and wet as she swept her lips across his face. She captured his lower lip between her teeth and sucked it into her mouth.

He pressed against her, his arousal heavy and aching with need. Maybe she wasn't as tired as he thought she was. Maybe they could share some more of that intoxicating passion before she went to sleep.

He laid her gently back onto the bed and joined her there after kicking off his shoes. She sprawled out beneath him, her body an open invitation, her smile a teasing come-on. He rained kisses across her face and down her chest until he reached those breasts. Those breasts.

He made quick work of the bra and tossed it in the vicinity of the chair. He buried his face between her breasts, reveling in their softness, their roundness, their fullness. He swept his mouth across them, lingering at the hard nipples. He took one of them into his mouth, suckling gently. Then as she arched against him and moaned, he sucked harder on the nipple, drawing it deeper into his mouth.

"Daniel," she murmured, wiggling beneath him. "Oh, yes, Daniel."

He reluctantly let go of her breasts. "I'm going to get out of these clothes."

She nodded and closed her eyes.

Daniel stood and tripped over the shoes he'd dropped. He cursed and kicked them across the room. They hit the wall with twin thuds. He unbuttoned his shirt and tossed it on top of Roxy's clothes. His pants, boxers and socks followed quickly. He took off his glasses and set them on the nightstand beside the bed.

He glanced over at Roxy as he reached down to turn off the light.

Her eyes were closed again. Her mouth hung slightly open. A soft snore escaped her lips.

Poor thing.

Daniel didn't know if he was referring to Roxy. Or himself.

He grabbed a blanket from the end of the bed and pulled it up over her bare body. Her beautiful bare body. She rolled onto her side and clutched the blanket to her.

He couldn't stop the long sigh that came from deep inside him. He stood for a moment, gazing at her. A flood of emotion washed over him.

He loved her.

When he had been looking for passion, he'd never expected to find love as well. This passionate woman who lived life to the fullest had pulled him right along with her. He couldn't imagine his life without her. How could he have ever thought that the world inside his lab was more exciting than the one outside?

Roxy murmured something in her sleep and turned over, exposing a portion of her luscious, behind. He pulled the blanket back over her, but not before he indulged in a loving stroke along her soft ass. He leaned over and placed a kiss on her silky hair.

Then he turned from the bed, put on his glasses and reached for his clothes.

Daniel carefully opened Roxy's bedroom door and slipped out quietly so he wouldn't wake her. She needed her sleep more than he needed to sleep with her. Although his body ached in disagreement. He gently closed the door behind him and was surprised to see Gina sitting on the sagging sofa in the living room.

She didn't seem surprised to see him. "Hey, Dr. Jennings."

"Hi, Gina." He nodded toward the bedroom door. "She's

asleep."

"Good. She's had a rough time of it."

Frankly, Gina appeared to have had a rough time too. At the very least, she appeared troubled. She was so tiny sitting cross-legged in the middle of that huge old sofa, looking a little lost. Since she was usually so upbeat, he was concerned to see her like that.

Daniel sat beside her and something, probably a spring, gave him a sharp jab in the ass. He winced and shifted his weight.

"Are you okay?" he asked.

Gina shrugged, but her gaze didn't meet his. "Got some stuff on my mind."

"Are you upset that I'm seeing Roxy?"

Her eyes grew wide. "Oh, no, Dr. Jennings. I think it's great."

That was a relief since she and Roxy were roommates. And she was his assistant. Things could have gotten very uncomfortable if she had a problem with him and Roxy. "I'm glad to hear that. Is everything okay at school?"

She picked at some invisible lint on her jeans. "Yeah, my classes are all going great. Hard to believe it's finally my last year."

"Your family all doing well?" He knew she came from a big, close, Italian family.

She smiled. "Oh, yeah."

"Plans coming together for work after graduation?"

She shrugged again. "I'm keeping my options open, but things are looking good. Really."

Daniel thought he'd done enough prying. "All right, then. I guess I'll head out." He walked toward the door. "Night, Gina."

"Um, Dr. Jennings?"

Daniel turned back to see uncertainty written on Gina's face. What could make her so nervous? "What is it?"

"Can I talk you to you about the potion?"

He froze. The potion! How could he have forgotten about the potion? He hadn't used the formula last night. He hadn't expected to find Roxy waiting for him when he got home last night, so he hadn't put on any of the formula before they wound up in bed together.

What did the last twenty-four hours mean in terms of his experiment?

More importantly, what did it mean that he found his passion without the benefit of the formula? That he'd fallen in love without using the *love potion*?

Roxy still wanted to make love with him tonight. How long had it been since he'd used the potion? What kind of scientist was he? He couldn't even remember. He had it written down in his notebook. He patted his pockets even though he knew he didn't have it with him. He used to carry his notebook with him always. He had to get home and record all his findings.

He was at the apartment door when he heard Gina stand. "Dr. Jennings?"

"Oh, I'm sorry, Gina. Can we talk later?" He knew she wanted to start trials and he still wasn't ready to admit to her that he'd been using it already. "I just remembered something important. I have to go."

He left the apartment. At first he was thrilled by the apparent fact that the formula hadn't worn off during the hours he hadn't been using it. Thrilled that Roxy was still attracted to him when he wasn't wearing the elixir.

But he was also concerned, because in the back of his

mind he knew he still had to admit to Roxy that he'd used a love potion to make her fall for him. And once she knew about the formula, how could she ever believe he really loved her?

Daniel came by the restaurant to drive Roxy home the next night. It was the only time he could see her, and he'd discovered that, elixir or no elixir, he needed to see her as much as possible.

Roxy glared at him as he walked in. What was that for? She finished pouring Charlie's coffee before she spoke to Daniel.

"I'm surprised to see you here," she said after he took the stool next to Charlie.

He said hi to Charlie and then feasted his eyes on Roxy. "Why are you surprised?"

Her pretty chin jerked up into the air. Was she really upset with him? "You left me last night."

"You fell asleep."

She blushed and glanced quickly at Charlie. She lowered her voice, although Charlie still would have had no trouble hearing her. "You could have woken me up."

"No, I couldn't. You needed your sleep."

She sighed. "I was pissed when I woke up and you were gone. You didn't even leave me a note."

"A note? What did you want me to say? Sleep tight?"

Charlie chuckled. "Don't let the bed bugs bite?"

"I let you sleep, Roxy. You needed it."

She dropped her annoyed tone. "I know. I just missed you."

"I've missed you all day long," he told her. "Are you about ready to leave?"

She shook her head. “Amy had to leave early. Sitter problems. I have to close up.”

“And I suppose you opened this morning?”

She shrugged and looked away. “More coffee, Charlie?”

“No, thanks,” he said. He reached for his wallet. “I’m headed back to the hospital to see Sandy before it gets too late. Good to see you, Daniel.”

“You too. How’s Sandy doing?”

“Holding her own, but the doctors aren’t as happy with her progress as they’d like to be. Guess she probably won’t be out for a few more days.”

After Charlie left, Daniel turned back to Roxy. He grabbed her hand. “Honey, I’m sure your mom will be fine.”

Roxy nodded. “I stopped in and saw her on my lunch break. She’s still pretty weak.”

“She’s at the best place she can be.”

“I know. I just worry.” She yawned. “Sorry.”

Those circles weren’t under her eyes a few days ago. “Roxy, you’re not going to be able to keep this up.”

“What do you mean?”

“Look at you. You’re dead on your feet. You’re here early in the morning until the middle of the evening. You ran to the hospital at your break instead of resting. You’re not going to have any energy to keep up on your classes.”

Much less spend time with him.

“I’ll manage. It’s just until Mom gets back on her feet.”

“Why don’t you hire someone else? A manager to cover for your mother, so you don’t work yourself to death. Another waitress or two.”

“I’m not working myself to death. We can’t afford to hire a

manager or more waitresses right now. The restaurant holds its own, but we don't have that kind of money."

"Let me help."

She grabbed a rag and started wiping down the counter. "What? You want to wait tables in between classes?"

"I can help you financially. I can help you get a manager for the restaurant."

Roxy glanced around as if she expected to find a hidden camera. Or someone listening in. There were no customers around them. "Why would you do that?"

How could she even ask that? "Because I love you. You mean the world to me and I don't like to see you so tired and working such long hours. I've got plenty of money to help you with the restaurant."

"Wait a minute." She dropped the rag and her eyes grew wide. "Back up. What did you say?"

"I said I have plenty of money. I—"

"No, back up farther. What did you say first?"

This wasn't going at all the way the way he'd planned. Of course, he hadn't planned to blurt it out like that. He reached out and took her hand. "I said I love you."

"Oh God." She yanked her hand away and starting pacing behind the counter. "Are you crazy?"

A cold wave washed over him. "Well, I didn't think so," he said wryly. "I guess I can assume that you don't love me back."

"Love." Roxy rolled her eyes. "I would think a man of science would know better than to buy into all the love bullshit."

He slowly rose to his feet, her rejection weighing heavily on his shoulders. "I love you, Roxy. It's not bullshit."

"You're just in lust," she said bitterly. "We're good in bed and you want more of that passion. Don't you, Daniel?"

Daniel couldn't deny that, but he knew it wasn't the only reason. "It's more than the sex."

"My father left my mom after he told her he loved her. Todd left me after he told me the he loved me too. Maybe they both thought they were in love in the beginning. I don't know about that. But I know it doesn't last."

"I'm not going anywhere, Roxy. Let me help you."

Roxy knew Daniel truly believed what he was saying. Now. Todd probably believed all the sweet and wonderful things he'd said to her in the beginning too.

Daniel's warm brown eyes gazed at her. She felt herself weakening. But as tempting as it was to take Daniel up on his offer of help, she'd never count on a man again.

She didn't love him. Could never love him. Damn it.

Daniel came around behind the counter and she was in his arms before she knew it. "Come on, Roxy. We're good together, you know we are."

She pressed her hips blatantly into his. "Yeah, we're good in bed together."

"That's not what I'm talking about and you know it."

She backed away and he let her go. "I have to do this myself, Daniel. I appreciate the offer, but I'll take care of it. I'll talk to Mom and we'll work it out."

"Sandy and Roxy against the world," Daniel said, his voice surprisingly bitter.

"What?"

"Something Charlie said to me," Daniel said. He shoved his hands in his pockets. "That it's always been you and your mom against the world and you don't let anyone else in."

"We've only had each other."

"Well, if you believe that, you're blind." There wasn't anything else he could say. With a rock sinking into the pit of his stomach, he turned and walked out the door.

Chapter Eleven

Roxy unlocked the door of the restaurant and flipped on the kitchen lights. She shut the door behind her and then dropped into the chair that sat against the wall. She sighed and closed her eyes.

It had been so hard to crawl out of bed and get going this morning. It was dark and cold and she felt like crap. Daniel had warned her about taking care of herself, but with her mom and the restaurant and trying to keep up with her classes, she simply didn't have the time to worry about herself.

Daniel. She'd barely seen him in the past few weeks. He probably thought she was avoiding him. But the truth was she missed him. Missed the puppy dog eyes behind the studious glasses. The playful heart behind the serious exterior. The warm hands and hot mouth. The man who saw her as she was and loved her anyway.

She groaned and dropped her head back against the wall. Why did he have to say he loved her? Why did he offer to help her? Sweep her up in his arms and take care of her?

Damn it, she didn't want a white knight to ride in and rescue her. She wanted to do it on her own. She wanted to take care of herself.

But she wanted Daniel too.

The door opened beside her and Jorge, the breakfast cook,

walked in. "Mornin', Roxy."

"Hey, Jorge, how's it going?"

The elderly man with tight white curls and graceful hands stopped in front of her, bending down to study her face. "I'm okay, sweetie, but you don't look so good."

People had been telling her that a lot lately. "No, I'm okay." If she said it enough, maybe she'd believe it.

"I think maybe you're working too hard."

What else is new?

She couldn't sit here all morning. There were things she had to do before she unlocked the front door. "Mom's going to come in for a few hours again today. I'll rest a little then."

Jorge shook his head, but didn't say anything else. He wrapped an apron around his waist and went about his morning routine.

Roxy made coffee and stocked the refrigerator case. She didn't have to wait tables in the morning. Joanne and Becky would be there any minute. She poured herself a cup of coffee and grabbed her algebra textbook.

She knew she was barely treading water as far as her classes were concerned. Actually, she was slowly drowning. Trying to keep up was turning into a losing battle. She'd missed so many lectures, she was completely lost when she tried to complete the homework assignments.

She was going to have to quit school. Just the thought shoved an ice pick through her stomach, but she couldn't see any way around it. It didn't help to say that she could go back again next semester. She was afraid she was lying to herself.

Roxy thought she was feeling a little better until Jorge started cooking bacon. Something in the greasy odor went straight to her stomach and flipped it over. She ran past Joanne and Becky to reach the restroom.

Throwing up coffee was not a pleasant experience. When she was finished, Roxy hung limply on sink and washed out her mouth. No wonder she felt awful. She must be coming down with that stomach flu that was going around. What other reason was there for being sick in the morning?

Another reason hit her upside the head. Roxy stared in horror at her reflection in the mirror above the sink. She backed up until she hit the wall behind her and then slid down to the floor.

Shit. When was her period due? Was it overdue? With all the stress of her mother's illness and everything else going on, Roxy honestly couldn't remember.

But she and Daniel had used protection, she'd made sure of it. The last thing she'd wanted in her life was an unplanned pregnancy. Especially now.

No. She couldn't be pregnant. She was jumping to conclusions. She had to have the flu. She was run down, just as Daniel had predicted. Her resistance was down. She probably picked up the flu bug from one of her customers.

She got to her feet, but the nausea rose in her throat again. She swallowed, hoping she wouldn't heave again. She sure didn't need morning sickness on top of everything else in her life.

She groaned with the realization that she was actually considering the fact that she might be pregnant. When she got her break, she was running down the street to the drug store. She didn't want to wonder whether or not her dreams were ruined.

She had to know for sure.

Blue for a boy, pink for a girl. No, it was blue for not pregnant, pink for a baby. Roxy huddled in the restroom of the restaurant and tried not to stare at the indicator. Was this like a watched pot never boiling?

She put down the seat cover and sat on the toilet to wait. The second hand on her watch seemed to crawl. She hoped none of her female customers had to use the restroom for the next few minutes.

Her hands shook. Why would life throw an unplanned pregnancy her way? Even though she knew condoms weren't foolproof, she'd been so careful. It wasn't fair.

Life wasn't fair. She'd heard that from her mother since she was a little girl.

What would Daniel think? He might believe that he loved her, but he never said anything about children. Roxy hugged her arms close around her, pressing against her queasy stomach. She glanced at her watch. It was almost time to check the indicator.

She'd never thought herself to be a coward, but she didn't want to look. She didn't want to know.

But deep down she already knew. She looked.

Pink.

Fuck.

She picked it up and threw it across the tiny room. It hit the wall and bounced back to smack into her shin. She cursed and threw it in the trash can.

Tears spilled down her face. There went *her* time. She'd end up working at the restaurant for the rest of her life, struggling to put a child through school, just like her mother did.

There went her dreams.

Just then a knock sounded at the door. A voice called out, "Is someone in there?"

"Just a minute," Roxy said, swiping at the tears still streaming down her cheeks. "I'll be right out."

She ran water in the sink and splashed some on her face. She dried her face and hands with some paper towels and dropped them into the trash can, covering up the pregnancy test. She took a deep breath. This was her life. She'd have to deal with it.

Daniel rubbed his eyes and tucked his notebook into the pocket of his lab coat. It was hard to believe he used to spend all his hours happily in this lab. Now the walls seemed to be closing in on him. He wanted nothing more than to stop by Roxy's restaurant and see how she was doing, but he'd promised himself he'd give her some time.

Deep down he supposed he'd been hoping she would come to him. Hoping she was going to realize she loved him too. Hoping they could look forward to a future full of passion together.

But he hadn't heard from her at all. It had been weeks. All Gina would tell him was that Roxy was working hard and trying to keep up with her schoolwork.

Had the potion's influence worn off? Not on his end, that was for sure. He hadn't used it since before that magical night they made love. He took the notebook out of his pocket to check the exact date and write down his speculations.

But before he could, the new cell phone in his pocket rang.

He fumbled the phone in his hurry to answer it. But one

glance at the number and he knew it wasn't Roxy. "Hello, Dad."

"It's your mother, Daniel."

"Oh, hi, Mom. How are you?"

"Fine. I'm calling with one last plea for you to come and work with your father and me."

Daniel started to refuse outright again, as he had countless times before. But this time he stopped. It wasn't because his mother called this time. It had more to do with feeling up in the air with his life at the moment. If Roxy didn't love him, did he want to hang around Cowden for the rest of his life?

"That job is still open, son, but it won't be for long," she went on. "You've seen the equipment we have here. And the funding is phenomenal. You could do so much more than you can where you are now."

"I know. But I'd miss the teaching."

"That's why I'm calling. They're willing to put you in charge of a new department. You'd be training new scientists, new hires, bringing them up to date on the equipment, the techniques. Then you'd get to start a new research project with them working under you."

Daniel listened. He couldn't help but get a little thrill at the thought of the opportunity his mother described to him. But did he want to leave the university? The students?

Or should the real question be, did he want to leave Roxy?

Her bright eyes shone in his mind. He felt her body pressed up against him as if she were right there in the room with him. He heard her laughter.

He heard her scoff at his declaration of love.

Maybe it was time to move on.

"We'd be proud to work with you, Daniel," his mother went on. "I know your father and I aren't the most demonstrative people, but we do love you. We would like to see you more often. Work with you. See what you can do to further medical science."

"Mom, I don't know..."

"This is an exciting place to work, son. I have all the confidence in the world in you. You could do amazing things here."

Was he really considering it? He had to see Roxy. He had to talk to her before he made a decision like this.

He sighed. "You're making a good case. Can I let you know in a few days?"

"Dr. Walters is retiring at the end of the month. We need to fill his spot as soon as possible. I don't know how much longer they'll wait."

Daniel took a deep breath. Would his mother understand? "There's this girl."

There was a short pause. "That's wonderful, Daniel." Her voice grew a little softer. "I'd love to meet her. Bring her with you."

"It's not that simple. Her mother is ill. She can't just pick up and leave."

"If she cares for you, she'll want what's best for you."

But what was best for him?

"I have to talk to her first. I'll call you in the morning."

Roxy waited tables all afternoon on autopilot. Her mind alternated between thinking about Daniel and thinking about the baby that even now was growing inside her. Gradually her anger had faded, replaced by a sense of awe. A baby. She was going to be a mother.

When things slowed down later in the evening, she poured a cup of tea and sat at the counter.

Of course, she'd wanted children. Just not right now. Sometime in the future, after she got her degree. God had a funny sense of timing.

"What's up?" Amy asked.

Roxy looked up from the cup of tea she'd been staring at for the past ten minutes. "What?"

"Dreaming about that handsome doctor?" Amy asked with a grin.

"He has been on my mind," Roxy admitted, not ready to admit the rest of it.

"Why haven't I seen him in here lately?"

"I kinda pushed him away." Now why did she admit that?

Amy waved her hand like a crazy person. "Why would you do that?"

"He told me he loved me." When Roxy said it out loud, it made her sound like a crazy person.

"Well, duh, anyone could see that."

Roxy stared at her. "Really?"

"Yeah. You should be happy! A good-looking, nice guy who happens to be a doctor tells you he loves you, and you push him away? Girl, what's wrong with you?"

"I don't know. He made me nervous, I guess. I don't know what to do with a nice guy."

"You thank God every day for him," Amy told her. "You certainly don't push him away."

"I was scared. My life is changing so fast and not at all in the way I thought it was going to."

"Yeah, life has a way of throwing you curve balls. But that doesn't mean you don't stay in the game."

"I take it the new guy you're dating is into baseball?"

Amy just laughed. The telephone rang and she picked up the receiver. "Sandy's Diner." She glanced over to Roxy. "Yeah, she's right here. Hold on." She handed Roxy the receiver, stretching the cord across the counter. "It's the nice guy."

Butterflies beat double time in her stomach. "Hey, Doc. You read my mind."

There was silence on the other end for a moment. She knew he didn't like her to call him Doc. Why did she keep doing it?

"Holding me at arm's length again?" He sounded stiff and cold.

"No, I'm sorry, Daniel. I get flip when I get nervous."

"Why are you nervous?" His voice only warmed up a couple degrees.

"I was just going to call you."

"Oh?" Still cold.

Oh, wow, this was hard. "Yeah, and I was trying to think of what to say but you beat me to it and I haven't had time to plan."

"Just talk to me, Roxy." His voice was softer now. Warmer. "You don't have to plan the words."

If he only knew what she had to tell him.

"I miss you," she said. "I want to see you."

She heard the big sigh through the phone line. She could almost feel the warm air on her face. "I want to see you too. That's why I called."

"It is?" Joy rushed through her veins. "When can I see

you?"

"Now. Anytime. When can you get away?"

"Soon, I hope."

"You want me to come pick you up?"

"No. I don't know how soon I can get away. I'll take a cab over to your place."

"I miss touching you," he said, his voice now slow and seductive. "I want to spend the entire night touching you."

His smooth voice slid like a warm caress across her skin. "I want that too."

"Your body is so soft, Roxy. I want to feel your softness pressed up against me. You don't know how I've missed holding you."

She glanced around her. There were a few other people at the counter and Amy was still standing in front of her. Roxy couldn't speak as candidly as Daniel could. "I've missed that too."

"I want to kiss you everywhere," he went on. "Your tasty lips, your silky skin." He paused for a second. "That soft center between your legs."

"Daniel!" she cried in a loud whisper. Warm tingles of awareness washed over her even as she felt her face heat up.

"What?" he asked with a chuckle. "Can anyone there hear me?"

"Well, no, but I just didn't expect you to say that."

"Why not?"

"I just didn't, that's all."

"Honey, I'm hard as a stone just thinking about it. Come over here as soon as you can."

"I will." She swallowed then told herself she couldn't wimp

out. "Daniel?"

"Yes?"

"We have to talk."

"Yes," he replied. "We do."

When had it started raining? The heavy downpour drummed on the roof of the taxi. Roxy stared out the window, watching the drops streak the glass. Her hands were clenched together and her stomach was tied in knots.

She was so looking forward to seeing Daniel again. To see his deep brown eyes and ready smile, to feel his arms around her again. But she was also nervous, afraid of how he was going to react to the news she had to tell him.

Daniel would be a wonderful father. She knew it. But he'd probably want to marry her right away. Should she agree for the baby's sake? Or should she stick to her guns and remain independent. In control of her life.

Ha. She didn't have control of anything.

The cab pulled up in front of Daniel's apartment building and after paying the driver, Roxy dashed out into the heavy rain. Joe, the security guard, must have been watching for her, because he pulled the door open just as she got there.

"Evening, Roxy," he said as she dashed past him into the dry, quiet lobby.

"Thanks, Joe." She looked at him through wet hair and tried to brush the worst of the water off her shoulders. "Forgot my umbrella."

"Dr. Jennings is expecting you. You can go right up."

"Thanks."

The elevator ride was over in an instant and she could see Daniel waiting at the door of his apartment when she stepped into the hallway. Her whole body seemed to fill with a sense of lightness. Of rightness. As if this was where she was supposed to be. As if Daniel was the one she was supposed to be with.

It was almost what she imagined love would feel like.

She stopped in her tracks a few feet from his door. Love, like in the movies? Like in happily ever after?

"Hey," he said softly. "Are you okay?"

She just stared at him, not able to move forward or backward. Too many things had happened. How many changes could one person take at one time?

"Roxy?" Daniel stepped out into the hallway. "Look at you, you're dripping wet." He reached her and put his arm around her. "Come on. Let's get you inside."

She let him lead her into his apartment. Her skin was chilled, her mind numb, her stomach clenched. She was still trying to wrap her mind around the thought that she had fallen in love with this man and she was having his baby.

He closed the door behind them, and then pulled her into his arms. She sank against him for a moment, savoring his touch, until she remembered how wet she was.

She pulled away. His shirt had dark, wet spots on it. "I'm getting you all wet."

He laughed. "That's all right." He cupped her face in his hand. "I've missed you." He kissed her once, a long, drawn-out brush of his lips across hers. "Let's get you out of these wet clothes."

She smiled and her mood lifted. "Ah, so that's the idea."

He brushed the wet hair out of her face and smiled back. "Well, I'd hoped to get you out of them sometime tonight, but the rain just played into my hands."

A chill ran through her from the wet clothing now plastered to her skin. Daniel quickly unbuttoned her shirt and pulled it off her body. Still standing on the tile floor in the foyer, Roxy quickly stripped off the rest of her clothing.

She stood naked before him. In every way possible.

Chapter Twelve

His eyes seemed to darken as he stared at her. He took her hand, his fingers warm against her chilled skin. “Follow me.”

He led her into his bedroom. The thick carpet was soft against her bare feet. He kissed her nose lightly. “Be right back.”

Roxy stood there, wet and naked in the middle of his bedroom. One glance at the bed and memories of making love here with Daniel came flooding back. It had been wonderful. He had been wonderful. Was it possible that she loved him even then and didn’t realize it?

Daniel came back into the room with a large, fluffy black towel.

She reached for it, but he grinned and kept his hold on it. “Allow me.”

She still wasn’t used to others doing for her, but she made herself ignore the instinct to snatch the towel out of his hand. She dropped her hands, stood there, silent and still, and let him dry her off.

He started with her head, patting the towel on her hair to soak up the worst of the water that had still been running onto her body. Then he began to rub the towel across her shoulders with long, brisk strokes. He continued down her back, the friction warming her as he rubbed the towel across her skin.

When Daniel reached her ass, she made herself stand there, proud and strong. Some of the derogatory comments Todd had made about the size of her butt echoed in her head, but she turned them off. And then as Daniel's strokes with the towel turned into caresses, all thoughts of Todd were wiped out of her mind. She could feel Daniel's hands through the thick towel, stroking her curves, rubbing down her thighs.

Shivers of desire began to spread through her body, warming her as surely as Daniel was warming her skin. She closed her eyes and let herself simply experience the pleasure of Daniel's pampering.

She felt him circle in front of her, but when he didn't start drying her off right away Roxy opened her eyes. He was staring at her with open desire on his face. At that moment she felt beautiful. She felt loved.

"You're perfect," he murmured. "Let me take care of these breasts for you." He began to rub the nubby fabric over her breasts, teasing her sensitive nipples, shooting sparks of need deep within her. She moaned and reached out to steady herself, grasping his strong shoulders.

Too soon, he left her breasts and continued down her body, skimming her stomach and then dipping between her legs. Her knees weakened with the pressure he applied there. If she hadn't already been holding onto his shoulders, she would have crumpled to the floor.

Daniel stepped closer to her, still rubbing the towel between her legs. "I don't know, sweetheart," he whispered in her ear. "I'm trying to dry you off, but I think you're just getting wetter and wetter."

He dropped the towel and she gasped when he plunged his fingers deep within her. "See, still wet."

"Daniel..." She couldn't find the words. She grabbed onto

his shoulders for support and brushed her lips across his throat. She wet his skin with her tongue and then scraped her teeth lightly along his skin.

He moaned then and, without warning, scooped her up into his arms. She laughed at the rush that swept through her body. He held her closely against him for a moment, and then strode over to the bed. He set her gently down on the mattress and then stepped back and just looked at her.

Roxy sat in the middle of the bed and enjoyed the view as she gazed back at him. At the man she loved. His hair was still shaggy. She'd have to get him over to see Heather at the Mane Event. She'd tell Heather not too short though. Roxy liked his hair long enough to comb her fingers through.

He wore a navy polo shirt tonight, tucked into a new pair of jeans they'd bought together that first weekend they'd met. The outfit showed his buff frame to perfection. No. It wasn't quite perfect.

She cocked her head. "Hey, this isn't fair." She got up on her knees. "You still have all your clothes on."

"I like looking at you," Daniel told her. "You're beautiful."

"Well, I like looking at you, too," she replied. She climbed off the bed. "I think it's time I took things into my own hands."

"Oh, really?"

She nodded. Grasping the hem of his polo shirt, Roxy pulled his shirt over his head. "Oh, yeah," she murmured. She spread her hands over his hard chest, tickling her palms with the coarse hair covering his sculpted muscles. She stepped forward and brushed her nipples against his chest. Oh, that felt so good, and from the expression in Daniel's dark eyes, he thought so too.

Roxy dropped to her knees and unbuckled his leather belt. She looked up at him and grinned before she took the zipper of his jeans in her hand. She covered him with her palm, feeling the hard ridge of his arousal through his jeans. He rocked his hips forward, pressing his thick shaft into her hand.

Roxy slowly lowered the zipper. The rasping sound was loud in the quiet surrounding them. She slid his jeans and briefs down his narrow hips and his erect penis sprang out in front of her face. He stepped out of his clothes and kicked them away.

Now that was perfect.

Still kneeling before him, she took his thick shaft into her hands. She could feel the strength there, the power. Yet when she took him deep into her mouth, she heard him moan and knew that right then she had all the power.

His hands grasped her head. His fingers tangled in her hair. She held the base of his cock and laved him with her tongue. He was salty and smooth beneath her tongue. The skin was so soft, the shaft so hard. She took him into her mouth again and moved slowly up and down along the length of him. Then faster. And deeper.

His fingers tightened on her hair. “Oh, Roxy. That’s wonderful, but I need you to stop that. Right now.”

She pulled back. “What’s wrong?”

“Nothing’s wrong. It’s very right. I just can’t take any more of that right now. I want this to last a little longer.” A wicked smile spread across his face. “And I want to come inside that hot, soft body of yours.”

“Oh.”

He took her by the shoulders and helped her to her feet. She grinned, reached out and took his glasses off. Then she put her hand on his chest and pushed him back onto the bed. After she placed his glasses on the nightstand, she crawled onto the bed beside him.

Before she knew what happened, she was on her back and Daniel was straddling her. His hard cock rubbed against her wet pussy, sending tingles everywhere along her body.

"God, I've missed you," he said. He kissed her hungrily, thrusting his tongue deep into her mouth. She sucked on his tongue and drank him in as if she were dying of thirst. She threw her arms around him, gathering him close.

She loved this man. The truth branded itself on her brain. It wasn't just that she craved his touch, although she certainly did. It wasn't just that she enjoyed being with him, even though that was true too.

She felt alive when she was with him. What could that be besides love?

Daniel nibbled on her lips. She tasted so sweet and fresh, like summer rain. He nipped at her throat, feasted on her breasts. He couldn't get enough of her taste. His body ached with urgent need, but he did his best to go slow, to show Roxy how precious she was to him. How much he cared about her. How glad he was to see her again.

Well, he was *very* glad to see her and his body wasn't going to let him forget it. His pulse began to throb thickly, the buzz in his body became more insistent, his cock ached with need.

He raised himself on his knees and looked down on her. Her hair was spread out on the pillow, her eyes were slightly unfocused. "Honey, I'm trying to go slow, but..."

"Slow? I don't need slow, Daniel." She wrapped her legs around him and pulled him to her. "I like it hard and fast. I like thinking you can't help yourself." She reached between them and put her hand around his thick cock. "I like knowing I did that to you."

His breath came out half gasp, half chuckle. "Oh, you did it all right." He leaned over and opened the drawer of his night stand. The rest of the condoms Roxy brought over were stashed in there. He grabbed one of the packets and tore it open. After rolling the latex protection over his cock, he turned his attention back to Roxy.

She guided him to her warm center. He slid easily into her, enveloped in her wet and ready flesh. She tightened her legs around him, reminding him that she didn't want slow and easy. Hard and fast worked for him too.

He moved in and out, building each stroke longer, harder, stronger. He knew he wouldn't last long this way, but he had hopes that this could be a very late night.

She moved under him, matching his rhythm. Her eyes were open, staring into his. Her breathing was ragged. He knew she was close to the edge so he reached between them and touched her sensitive bud.

She gasped. Her body bucked beneath him. He felt her muscles squeeze his cock and that was his undoing. He followed her over the edge, spiraling out of control, until he collapsed on top of her.

A few moments later, he felt Roxy move beneath him. He was probably crushing her. He lifted himself off her body and settled on the bed beside her. She tucked herself against him and placed her head on his shoulder.

"Mmm," she murmured, snuggling her body even closer. "I love you."

The warm contentment he'd been feeling simply washed away. He felt chilled and gathered her closer to him. "Did I hear you right?"

She nodded, her chin rubbing against his shoulder. "Yes, Daniel, do you want to hear it again? I love you."

Why didn't the words fill him with joy? Wasn't this exactly

what he'd been hoping for? "I thought you didn't believe in love?"

She raised her head off his shoulder and smiled at him. "I guess that was because I hadn't met you yet."

Beautiful words. What person wouldn't want to hear them?

There was a voice inside of him that was telling him to just rejoice in her declaration. Be glad in it and go on from here. She'd never know. No one would ever know.

But there was another voice that told him what they had would never be real if he didn't tell her about the potion. And damn, if that wasn't the voice he listened to. He groaned and sat up.

"What is it?" she asked. She frowned and sat up also.

"I have a confession to make."

She pulled the corner of the blanket up to her neck, covering herself. "Then go see a priest."

"No, this is something I have to tell you. Um, it's something I've wanted to tell you about for a while, but I didn't know how to do it."

She shifted away from him. "What? Do you have a wife and family on the other side of the country?"

"No! Why would you say a thing like that?"

"I'm trying to think of what could be so horrible that it would put that stricken look on your face."

"I don't have a wife and children."

"You're gay?"

He glanced at the tangled bedclothes and lifted his brows. "How can you ask that?"

"Well, tell me, so I don't have to guess."

How did he start? How did he make her understand?

"Roxy, I'm a scientist."

She sighed. "I know that."

"Scientists perform experiments. They conduct research."

"Like for that protein supplement you developed."

He allowed himself a little hope. Maybe she would understand. "Right. But, you see, the reason I wanted to develop a supplement like that was because I was a real geek in high school."

"You were?"

"Yeah, typical nerd. Skinny and brainy. Glasses and no dates."

"So you figured out how to make yourself buff?"

"Something like that."

She leaned closer to him again. "I can understand that. You wanted to be able to control how you looked. You made it happen. I think that's great."

"Um, thanks."

She snuggled up against him and let the blanket slip down enough to uncover the tops of her breasts. "Is that what you wanted to tell me?"

"No, not exactly." He swallowed. He cleared his throat. "I've been working on a new formula."

"Another body-building formula?"

"No. A pheromone-enhancing formula."

She wrinkled her nose. "Pheromone? I've heard that word before. What is it?"

"Basically pheromones are natural scents found in all animals and humans that can affect behavior, including sexual attraction."

"Sexual attraction?" Suspicion laced her voice.

He nodded and wished he'd never started this conversation. "When you came into my lab that first night, I had just started trials."

She pulled away from him again. "What does that mean, started trials?"

"I had just put on some of the potion when you came into the room that night. I hadn't expected to run into anyone while I was using it."

"Potion? You call it a potion?"

"Actually, Gina is the one that calls it a love potion."

"Love potion?" Roxy jumped out of bed and ran out of the bedroom.

Daniel followed her down the hall. "Roxy, listen to me."

She started to gather up her clothes from the foyer. "You used a love potion on me?"

"I told you I didn't know anyone was going to come into the lab. I certainly didn't know you were going to be there."

She glared at him as she stepped into her wet jeans. "That's why you took me out to eat, isn't it? That's why you asked me all those questions about if I was attracted to you." She gasped. "You took notes!"

"Roxy, try to understand. Once the experiment was started, I had to follow through."

"Did you use it again?"

He was silent as he watched her struggle to pull the wet denim up her legs. He knew she'd fight him if he tried to help her.

She'd fight him every step of the way.

She finally got them over her hips. "I asked if you used the love potion again when we were together." Her voice was low and cold.

"Yes."

"And kept track of my reactions in that little notebook of yours?"

"And my reactions too," he was quick to add.

She clutched her shirt to her chest, covering her breasts. "You used me. You experimented on me, like...like a lab rat."

Her words cut deep. "No, Roxy."

"I worked so hard to finally have control over my life. And now I find out I had no control over my own emotions." She struggled to straighten out her wet, twisted bra and then threw it against the wall in obvious disgust. She plunged her arms into the sleeves of her shirt. "And I really thought I'd fallen in love with you." She rolled her eyes. "What a fool I was. I knew better."

"Roxy, please, let me tell you about the rest."

She buttoned her shirt with shaky hands. "I can't take any more, Daniel. To find out you manipulated my emotions..." The last word came out with a sob.

"No, Roxy. I love you."

She glared at him. "Hey, Doc, how could you ever know for sure if it was me? Or the potion."

Scooping up her shoes, she turned away from him and walked out the door. Daniel didn't try to follow her. After the door slammed behind her, he walked back into the bedroom and sank onto the bed. One look at the tangled sheets made him feel as if he'd been socked in the stomach.

She was right. He did manipulate her emotions. And his own.

He wished he'd never told her, but she was right about something else. How could they ever be sure if they truly loved each other? If he'd never said anything, would they have woken up one day after the effects of the potion wore off and wondered what they were doing together?

He stood and paced the apartment, feeling his life fall apart around him. He walked over to where Roxy's bra still lay on the floor by the front door. He picked it up and rubbed the soft lace against his cheek. It smelled like Roxy.

Why did he waste his time trying to develop a stupid formula like this? Didn't he know that the real thing was all that mattered? If he couldn't find real passion that didn't have to be enhanced, it wasn't worth having.

When he got to the lab in the morning, he was going to destroy everything to do with the formula.

And tonight he was going to talk to his mother.

Chapter Thirteen

When Roxy got back to her apartment, the first thing she did was walk past Gina and crank up the radio. Then she sank onto the sofa next to Gina and clenched her shaking hands in her lap.

"Uh, oh," Gina said, raising her voice to be heard over Pat Benetar screaming "Heartbreaker". "Did you and Dr. Jennings have a fight?"

Roxy felt bruised and battered. And they'd only fought with words. "I need to talk to you."

"You're all wet."

She didn't even notice it anymore. "I'll change in a minute. I just have to talk."

"Okay, then I have to turn down this music." Gina got up and turned the radio down to its original volume. "I don't want everyone down the block to hear this." She plopped down beside Roxy. "Okay, what is this?"

"I'm pregnant." The words echoed in her ears. It was the first time she'd said the words out loud. It sounded all too real.

"Wow. Are you okay?"

Roxy shrugged. "I'm still trying to get used to the idea."

"How did it happen? I mean, you're smart enough to use protection, right?"

"Of course. I brought the condoms. I had them in the nightstand."

"And how old were they?"

"How old? I don't know. Todd probably bought them years ago. You mean those things have expiration dates?"

"I'm sure they have a shelf-life."

"Shit. Figures I'd use old condoms."

"What did Dr. Jennings say when you told him? Wait a minute, he didn't do something stupid like tell you he didn't want it or something."

"I haven't told him," Roxy admitted.

"Yet. Right?" Gina asked, the words slow and distinct. "You haven't told him *yet*."

"Yeah, I know I'm going to have to tell him eventually, but right now I never want to see him again, so that's going to make it a little difficult."

"What happened?"

She shivered and told herself it was from the wet clothes. "Let's just say he's not the person I thought he was."

"And here I thought he was a nice guy."

"Yeah."

"What are you going to do?"

"Handle it." She picked up one of the school books from the coffee table and rubbed her hand over the cover. "First, I'm going to quit school."

"Oh no, Roxy. Are you sure?"

"Yeah. I've been thinking about it for a while now anyway. Mom's not going to be able to work the hours she used to for a long time. Maybe not ever. I just can't keep up with the diner and school too." Tears sprung to her eyes, but she brushed them away before they could fall down her cheeks. “And I’m not going to be able to go to college with a baby, so, there’s no point in struggling with it now.”

“Lots of women with babies go to college.”

She was so tired and hurt she couldn’t even think straight. “I just can’t do it all right now.”

Gina leaned over and hugged Roxy. “It’ll all work out. I’ll help you all I can. But, hon, you need to talk to Dr. Jennings.”

“The thing is, I thought I really loved him. And he made me feel like a fool.”

“Why? Did he say he didn’t love you?”

“Oh, no. He told me he loved me too. But it was all because of a stupid love potion. Can you believe that?”

“The potion?” Gina’s voice rose about three octaves. “He said he used the potion?”

“Do you mean you knew about it?”

“Well, yeah, I’m his lab assistant. We’ve been working on the formula together for a while now, but I didn’t know he started using it. I can’t believe he started using it and he didn’t tell me. And I definitely didn’t know he used it on you.”

“Well, he did. On the night we met. So that magnetic pull I was trying to ignore wasn’t because I was really attracted to Daniel. It was because of the potion.” Just the thought caused an ache to spread within her. “And he kept using it every time we were together.”

Gina frowned and stood. “Oh, boy. I need to talk to Dr. Jennings.”

Roxy watched her pace back and forth across the small living room. “What is it, Gina?”

“Don’t give up on Dr. Jennings, Rox. Things aren’t always what they seem to be. Remember, he is the baby’s father. He’s going to be a part of your life, whether you want him to be or not."

Roxy brought her feet up onto the sofa cushion and wrapped her arms around her knees. Gina was right. Daniel would surely want to be a part of their child's life. Roxy couldn't deny him that. But how could she look at him again without remembering how he manipulated her and took her control away from her?

She stood. "I better get changed and go tell my mom."

When Roxy left the apartment, she saw Mr. and Mrs. Campbell coming up the walk. She paused at the bottom of the stairs and watched them from the shadows. Mrs. Campbell's hip must have been bothering her, because she was limping and leaning on her husband as they walked. His arm was wrapped around her waist as he helped her along.

He must have noticed Roxy standing there. He waved to her and called out her name.

She left the shadows and stepped into the moonlight. "How was bingo?"

"I won!" Mrs. Campbell exclaimed. "Two hundred dollars."

"Wow! That's great. What are you going to do to celebrate?"

"Oh, I don't know." She giggled. "Plan how I want to spend the money."

Mr. Campbell leaned over and whispered something in her ear. She blushed and slapped him on the shoulder. "Hiram!" She laughed out loud.

He winked at Roxy and then looked her over and frowned. "Are you okay? You working too hard again?"

"I'm fine. You guys go celebrate. I'm off to visit my mom."

"You give her my best," Mrs. Campbell said. She squeezed her husband's arm and they continued to the house, side by side, in a coordinated rhythm they must have learned through the years they'd spent together.

A bittersweet smile lifted her lips as a rush of longing ran through her. Some people were lucky. She'd never been one of the lucky ones.

Roxy was surprised when Charlie answered the door of the mobile home her mother lived in. She knew he spent a lot of time with her mother, especially since her heart attack, but it was pretty late.

Her mother was sitting in a new recliner. "See what Charlie bought me."

It was plush green and looked super comfortable. "It's very nice."

"But he insists we go for a walk everyday before I can sit in it." Her mother looked at Charlie and the expression on her face seemed to go beyond fondness. Beyond friendship.

"A bribe." Roxy winked at Charlie. "Good idea."

"What are you doing here so late?" Sandy asked. "You should be in bed. You need your rest."

"I have news."

"I have news too," her mother said. "Wouldn't it be amazing if we had the same news?"

"That would be incredible," Roxy replied dryly.

Her mother tilted her head and stared at Roxy's hands. "No engagement ring, so I guess our news isn't the same."

"Engagement ring?" Roxy cried. Her eyes darted from her mother to Charlie and back again. "Ok, guys, spill."

"Your mother finally agreed to marry me," Charlie said. He took her mother's hand and kissed it softly, tenderly.

Her mother held out her other hand and, sure enough, she wore an amazing diamond solitaire. “Oh, I’m so happy for both of you. I can’t believe it.” She hugged her mother and then Charlie.

“After my heart attack I realized that life is short and I didn’t want to live the rest of it alone. I don’t have to do it all alone. I can share the good times and the bad times. I can share the fun and the work.” She looked at Charlie with that love-struck expression again. “And I realized I loved this stubborn old guy.”

Roxy saw the way her mother and Charlie looked at each other and could almost believe in love.

Almost.

“What’s your news?” her mother asked.

“Um, I’m quitting school.”

She expected her mother’s *I told you so* look, but it didn’t come. Sandy pushed herself out of her recliner and put her arms around Roxy. “I’m so sorry, honey. You were working so hard. I know this is because of me.”

Roxy shrugged and hugged her mom back. “I can go back again later.”

“I’ve decided to take early retirement and help out at the diner,” Charlie told her. “We’ll get you back in classes next semester.”

Roxy nodded. There’d be time for the baby news soon enough. She gave them each a hug and kiss and left them to each other.

The next afternoon Roxy took some time off and went to the business office at the university. She expected to be depressed when she withdrew from all her classes. She was surprised at the relief that ran through her instead.

Maybe her mother was right after all. She needed to bloom where she was planted. She had to be happy with herself before the rest of her life could make any sense.

That didn't mean she shouldn't aim for something better. She was going to be an example of strength and persistence to this little one. It might take her a little longer to reach her goals, but she'd make it. Hell, maybe her goals would even change, but that would be okay, as long as they were right for her.

Like Daniel.

No. Daniel wasn't right for her. She glanced around as she left the building, so afraid she was going to run into him on campus. She knew she was being a coward. He deserved to know about the baby, but she couldn't bear to think about being so close to him and not wanting to touch him. To see those magical lips and remember how they felt against her skin.

She stomped down the sidewalk, reminding herself that he'd used her every bit as much as Todd had. Todd had used her to get his education. Daniel had used her for his research.

Would she ever be loved and needed simply for who she was?

Restless, she walked along the sidewalks with no real direction in mind. The exercise felt good. Fallen leaves crunched under her feet. The autumn air was crisp and refreshing.

Was it fate that brought her to the little shop filled with baby items? She stepped through the door and the air smelled soft and sweet. She stepped up to a table covered in tiny little outfits. Soft pinks and blues and greens and yellows. Roxy hesitantly reached out and picked up a little one-piece outfit.

It was so small. So soft. Roxy tried to imagine a baby that tiny. Her hand flew instinctively to her stomach. How tiny was her baby right now? She'd called the doctor and scheduled her first prenatal exam. The whole thing was suddenly becoming more real.

Raising a child on her own wouldn't be easy, but she knew it could be done. Her mother had managed to raise her and run a restaurant, and she'd survived. Roxy could do it too.

A table of beautiful blankets caught her eye, soft fleece in the colors of the rainbow. Roxy put the outfit back and walked over to the long table. She swept her hand over the blankets and then picked up a pale lavender one. She held it to her chest as an unexpected emotion swept over her.

Love.

She was going to wrap her baby in this blanket. She'd carry him or her home from the hospital nestled in soft lavender. The baby would be loved and cared for, she could promise that.

Roxy sank into a chair tucked into a corner. Soft music tinkled in the background, like a lullaby for her soul. She loved this little being growing inside her. This new person she and Daniel created together. She didn't know yet whether it was a boy or a girl. She didn't know what color the eyes or hair would be. She didn't know much at all, except that she loved this little one with all her heart.

She gasped and dropped the blanket into her lap as a thought came to her so profound, yet so simple, she should have realized it earlier.

If she loved this child she didn't yet know, how could she doubt the love she thought she felt for Daniel? How could she doubt the fact that real love existed? She saw it in the faces of her mother and Charlie. With Mr. and Mrs. Campbell. Some men did stick around. Instead of looking at her father and Todd as examples, she should have been looking at Charlie and Mr. Campbell. And Daniel.

She loved this baby and she loved its father. She knew it with every part of her body, with every bit of her soul.

If Daniel thought it was a stupid love potion that attracted her to him, he was dead wrong. It was those brown puppy dog eyes and that magnificent body. It was his warmth and caring, his need for passion and his toe-curling kisses. It was the driving her home after dark and the dancing in the little restaurant and the making out in the parking lot. It was so many things that made Daniel who he was. And who made him the man she loved.

None of that had anything to do with a chemical formula. But being a scientist was also part of the man she loved. She shouldn't be upset because he was doing his job. He couldn't stop trying to discover and research and experiment. It was part of who he was.

He'd wanted to explain and she hadn't let him. He told her about the potion because he was a good and honest man. He could have played it safe and never told her. She'd have never known the difference. He had to have been concerned that she would have reacted exactly how she did.

Still not really believing in love, she'd taken the easy way out. She'd pushed him away rather than staying and working it out. Rather than admitting not everything was within her control. And that she didn't have to do it all alone, whether it was running the restaurant, or raising a child, or simply living day to day.

A soft, middle-aged woman came over to her. "Are you all right?" The concern on her face made Roxy smile.

"I think everything is finally very all right." She stood and held out the lavender blanket. "I'd like to buy this. My first purchase for my baby."

She glanced at her watch and was surprised by how late it

was. Daniel should be home by now. She'd stop by right now and apologize. He was a smart man. He'd realize she pushed him away because she was afraid.

Darkness had fallen, but she saw that she was only a couple blocks from Daniel's building. She wondered if that's where she'd been heading all afternoon. Her steps almost bounced. Her mood was light for the first time in days.

Joe was sitting behind the desk in the lobby. She smiled as she walked up to him.

"Hey, Joe. Is Daniel home?"

"No, Roxy. I haven't seen him tonight. Maybe he's still at the college."

She nodded. "Thanks, Joe. I'll stop by there. Can you call me a cab?"

"Sure, Roxy." Joe reached for the phone. "We're sure going to miss him around here."

Roxy froze. "Miss him?"

"Well, I heard he's going to keep his lease, but I'm sure he won't be here very often once he takes that job in Philadelphia."

She was proud of how calm she sounded as she said, "I haven't seen Daniel in a few days. I didn't know he'd decided to take the job." *What job?*

Joe nodded. "The university will be sorry to see him go, I'm sure, but he'll be working with his parents, doing medical research. That's an important job."

"Yes, it is," she replied automatically. Her brain felt like mush, her heart hollow. He was leaving.

Well, she'd really screwed things up. She'd pushed him away from her for good.

He didn't love her enough to stay and try to work it out. Or maybe he'd figured he'd tried enough. She sure hadn't given him any indication he had a chance.

Her hands began to shake and she clasped them behind her back so Joe wouldn't notice. What was she going to do now? Was she going to hunt him down and beg? Or go home and cry herself to sleep?

"Hey, Joe. Can you call me that cab?"

The mess seemed to be growing around him, as if it were alive. Daniel stood in front of his desk and shook his head. The Blob, that's what it was. Oozing around him in all directions. His mind wasn't really on it. That was his problem.

Or one of them.

How could an attempt to organize his papers turn into this much chaos? He should have given the job to Gina. He glanced at his watch. How had it gotten so late? What was he going to do with this mess?

He gathered up the highest pile of papers. Pheromone research.

"Hey, Doc, what'cha doin'?" Roxy's sassy voice came from behind him.

He didn't look up from the papers in his hand, but he gave a big sigh of relief.

"Where have you been?" He tossed the papers in the trash can before he turned around to look at her. She stood in the doorway. She looked wonderful with that body he could sink into. The curves he loved to hold onto. He felt as if it had been years since he'd seen her instead of a day.

She shoved her hands into the pockets of her red coat and leaned against the doorjamb. "What do you mean where have I been? Working, where else?

"Not this afternoon. You weren't at the restaurant. You weren't at your apartment. No one knew where you were."

She didn't answer his question, but she did straighten up and walk into the room. "Well, you look like you got your hands full here. Moving out, I hear."

"Gina told me you quit school. I wish you hadn't done that."

"Yeah, well, I wish I didn't have to sleep, but I just don't have time for everything, Doc."

He'd let the Doc comment go this time. He understood she was still upset with him for using the potion and not telling her about it. He couldn't blame her.

But he'd been worried about her. "Why don't you carry a cell phone?"

"I can't afford one."

"I'll buy you one."

"Why? So you can call me from Philadelphia once in a while?"

"Who told you I was going to Philadelphia?"

"Joe, the security guard at your building."

"Joe shouldn't listen to rumors."

Roxy's eyes widened. "You're not leaving? You're not going to work with your parents on medical research?"

He took heart in the joy he thought he heard in her voice. "I thought about it. But I like my job here."

She took a couple steps closer to him. "I know you do. I'm glad you do."

"I also wasn't about to give up on you."

"You weren't?"

He shook his head and took a couple steps closer to her. "I

love you, how could I give you up without a fight?"

"I couldn't give you up either." Tears glittered in her eyes. "I'm sorry I didn't believe in love. I'm sorry I didn't believe in you."

"I have a confession to make," he said.

She rolled her eyes, even as tears slipped from them. "Another one?"

"Gina came to me today and admitted that she'd been trying out the formula too."

"You're kidding? She never said a thing."

"That's probably because she knew I wouldn't be happy with her. But after you told her I'd been using it, she broke down and told me. And guess what?"

"I have to guess?"

He laughed out loud. God, how he'd missed her sass. "It didn't work for her. Not at all. I guess she tried with a number of subjects."

"Oh. That's why she was going on so many first dates."

"Evidently. We went over our data today and came to the conclusion that the formula is flawed and I'll have to go back to the drawing board if I want to continue the research." He took her into his arms. He couldn't bear not to hold her any longer. "I threw away the drawing board. I think it's in this mess somewhere."

"You don't want to find a love potion?"

He shook his head. "Passion worth having is worth searching for. It's worth fighting for." He kissed the tip of her nose. "You know what this means, don't you?"

"What?"

"We came up with that attraction all on our own."

"Of course we did," she said, squeezing him tight. "Do you think you can bottle what we have?"

"Not a chance."

She backed slowly out of his embrace. "I have something to tell you too. I'm not sure how you're going to feel about it because it's certainly not something we ever discussed."

Now she was making him a little nervous. She was so serious. "What is it?"

"Remember the first night we made love at your apartment?"

"It's engraved in my memory."

"Well, evidently we used an old condom."

"Old condom?"

"As in ancient. Not sturdy. Leaky."

His heart started pounding so hard he wasn't sure he heard correctly. "Roxy, are you saying...?"

She nodded, an unsure look on her face.

"You're pregnant?"

She nodded again.

He stepped close to her and placed his hand over her stomach. "My child is in there?"

"Our child."

"Wow, our child." He threw his arms around her and swung her around the center of the room. "That's amazing. Wow." He stopped and looked at her, not sure by the expression on her face what she was feeling. "And how do you feel about this? I know it will throw a little detour in your plans, but we can make it work, Roxy. I know we can."

"I'm getting used to the idea."

He looked at all the papers strewn around them. "Can you

help me a minute? I seem to have lost something."

"Sure. What is it?"

He caught Roxy's hand and dropped down onto one knee. "My passion. I can't find it when I'm not with you. Please marry me, Roxy. We can be a family and work out things together. The restaurant, our baby, your education, my passion. We can do it all if we're in it together."

She laughed and pulled him up, into her arms. "Yes, I'll marry you." She nodded toward the piles of papers. "You need someone to take care of you."

"And you need someone to take care of you."

She didn't get defensive this time, but snuggled up to him. "And we'll take of the little one together."

Their lips met then, sealing their promise to each other. To take care of each other. And to keep the passion growing.

About the Author

To learn more about Natasha Moore, please visit www.natashamoore.com. Send an email to Natasha Moore at natasha@natashamoore.com or join her Yahoo! group to join in the fun with other readers as well as Natasha Moore!

http://groups.yahoo.com/group/natashamoore

There's more to life than playing make believe.

The Role of a Lifetime

© 2008 Jennifer Shirk

Sandra Moyer has a good reason to distrust actors. She was once married to one who left her and her child. However, she's desperate for publicity to help her struggling preschool. Hollywood playboy Ben Capshaw's request to access her classes to prepare for a role is an offer she can't refuse.

Sandra second guesses herself on that decision until she sees Ben in action with the children. Her apprehension turns to wonder, and then to feelings she'd thought were closed off forever. Yet how can she trust that what she's seeing is real?

As a boy, Ben learned that acting was the answer to everything. The role he's up for now will enhance his career and, he's sure, secure his happiness. But spending time with Sandra and her daughter stirs up emotions that—for once—aren't pretend.

Ben's ready for a lifetime role as husband and father—if he can convince Sandra not to typecast him.

She's in for the ride of her life

The Ride of Her Life

© 2007 Natasha Moore

After a devastating diagnosis, sensible Sarah Austin yearns to live life to the fullest. When she talks her former teenage crush into a cross-country ride on his Harley, she thinks it's her one and only chance for adventure, including a fun fling with Love 'em and Leave 'em Bastian.

No longer a rebel, Dean Bastian is a counselor for troubled teens and ready to settle down. He doesn't know why Sarah is so desperate for an adventure, but he's willing to do anything to keep a smile on her face, even pretend to still be a bad boy.

Sarah doesn't want to burden anyone with the future she faces, but can Dean convince her that the rest of her life can be an adventure...with him?

Enjoy the following excerpt from The Ride of Her Life...

"So, Dean, got some special girl waiting for you at one of your ports of call?" Her voice was soft again, almost tentative.

"All women are special as far as I'm concerned," he said. "But only one? Not a chance."

"Yeah, that's what I thought. Same old Dean. Did you know they called you Love 'em and Leave 'em Bastian back in high school?"

He winced at the reminder. It may have been true—hell, it *still* was true—but that didn't mean he liked the name. It implied some callousness on his part, and he'd always been very careful about the women he got involved with, even in high school. He'd parted friends with every one of them. They usually ended up feeling sorry for him because he had a character flaw that made him unable to get serious about any one woman.

"Yeah, I knew that, but I didn't know you knew that."

"Oh, sure I did." But there wasn't sarcasm or disgust in her voice like he thought there might be. If he didn't know better, there seemed to be a touch of affection in her voice. She gathered up her book and sunglasses and started to stand up. She groaned and wobbled a little, leaning back against the tree. After she dropped what she was holding, she grabbed her butt and slid back down to the ground.

"Are you okay?" he asked.

"You may be used to sitting on that bike all day, but I'm not. I'm a long way from having an iron butt."

He chuckled lightly. "You'll get used to it." Then before he could think about all the reasons he shouldn't, he said, "Lie down on your stomach."

She looked up at him and frowned. "What?"

“Lie down on your stomach,” he repeated. He knew he would regret doing this, but he’d already knelt beside her. “I think a massage is in order.”

Her eyes widened. “You’re going to massage my butt?”

“Do you want to feel better or not?”

“Oh, yeah.” She grinned. “I just wanted to make sure that’s really what you had in mind.”

He knew he was in deep trouble, but he made himself smile back. He took the sleeping bag she’d been sitting on and spread it out beneath the tree. She lay down on her stomach, her denim-clad legs and bottom stretching out beside him. She cradled her head on her arms and looked back at him.

“Okay. I’m ready.”

Dean was glad for the darkness that finally enveloped their campsite. The campfire light flickered over them. His heart beat in a matching, uneven rhythm. He flexed his fingers and imagined touching her. He reached out his hands and held them in the air, suspended over her tight buns. What did he think he was doing? How could he touch her there, of all places, and not want to touch her everywhere else?

And how could he not want to make love with her before they were done?

Hell, wanting had never been the problem. Controlling that desire was where he had his difficulty.

“Dean?”

She was still lying there, willing to submit to his attention. Trusting him to make her feel better. He was simply going to massage her sore and tired muscles. That’s all. He could do this. And to prove it to himself, he lowered his hands to the shapely denim.

Soft, yet firm. Hard, yet yielding. Dean rubbed and kneaded

the knotted muscles and tried to put sweet little Sarah out of his mind. He was simply massaging some aching muscles. He was giving aid where it was needed.

He was so hard it hurt.

Sarah moaned and shimmied closer to him. "Oh, yes," she murmured. "Yes, right there. Oh, that feels incredible."

He swallowed and shifted position to try to relieve some of the pressure on his zipper. She was killing him, but he kept it up, massaging the tense muscles in her thighs and buttocks. He tried to focus his attention on his hands and watch them rather than looking at Sarah.

What a joke. From the glow of the fire he could see her. Not the details, not the little things that didn't matter right now, but her shapely body as a whole. The way her hips curved out just enough to make them hips, a woman's hips. The way her waist narrowed and her shoulders gracefully broadened, supporting the slender neck that he could admire now that her hair was short. And her ears, so delicate, and though he couldn't see them now, he could picture the little gold balls he'd noticed earlier decorating the lobes.

"Um, Dean?"

Sarah's voice brought him back from his musings about her body. He noticed that his massaging strokes had slowed down and deteriorated into something more like a grope. He snatched his hands away.

"Sorry."

She sat up close beside him, too close. "That's okay," she said. "Thank you. That was wonderful. I feel a lot better."

She looked at him for a moment, as if she expected him to say something or do something. He wished he knew what she was thinking and what she wanted him to do.

"Well, I think I'm going to turn in," she said finally, her voice soft, almost seductive. She picked up her journal and the sunglasses. "You coming?"

That certainly sounded seductive. Dean looked at the little tent. What had he been thinking? There was no way he was crawling in there with her now. He'd never be able to sleep lying close enough to her that their breaths would mingle in the darkness. How would he ever avoid touching her, smelling her, pulling her into his arms and burying his body deep inside hers?

He jumped to his feet. "I'm going to sleep out here." He picked up the second sleeping bag and spread it out on the other side of the campfire.

She slowly got to her feet and walked over to him. She placed her hand on his arm. It felt as if a spark from the fire had landed there. "What if it rains tonight? There's plenty of room in the tent for both of us."

He looked up at the darkened sky. Bright stars twinkled through the smattering of clouds. "It's not going to rain," he said. "I told you I like to be outdoors. I always sleep in the fresh air. I only brought the tent along for you to sleep in."

Without warning, she reached out and brushed a hand as soft as velvet across his cheek. A smile slowly spread across her face. "Do I make you nervous, Dean?"

Her eyes glowed from the reflection of the flames. He wished he could lie to her, pretend he was unaffected by her being there, only a heartbeat away. But he'd already told her too many lies.

Smoke from the campfire swirled around them, making it hard for him to breathe. "You make me real nervous, Sarah," he replied. Why did his voice suddenly sound so ragged? It must have been the smoke.

She leaned forward and brushed her lips lightly across his. "I liked kissing you," she whispered, her lips moving against his. "Kiss me again, Dean."